PUFFIN CLA

The Best of Tenida

The Best of Tenida

NARAYAN GANGOPADHYAY

Translated from the Bengali by Aparna Chaudhuri

Introduction by Sampurna Chattarji

PUFFIN BOOKS

PUFFIN BOOKS

Published by the Penguin Group

Penguin Books India Pvt. Ltd, 11 Community Centre, Panchsheel Park,
New Delhi 110 017, India

Penguin Group (USA) Inc., 375 Hudson Street, New York,
New York 10014, USA

Penguin Group (Canada), 90 Eglinton Avenue East, Suite 700, Toronto,
Ontario, M4P 2Y3, Canada (a division of Pearson Penguin Canada Inc.)

Penguin Books Ltd, 80 Strand, London WC2R 0RL, England

Penguin Ireland, 25 St Stephen's Green, Dublin 2, Ireland
(a division of Penguin Books Ltd)

Penguin Group (Australia), 707 Collins Street, Melbourne, Victoria 3008,
Australia (a division of Pearson Australia Group Pty Ltd)

Penguin Group (NZ), 67 Apollo Drive, Rosedale, Auckland 0632,
New Zealand (a division of Pearson New Zealand Ltd)

Penguin Group (South Africa) (Pty) Ltd, Block D, Rosebank Office Park,
181 Jan Smuts Avenue, Parktown North, Johannesburg 2193, South Africa

Penguin Books Ltd, Registered Offices: 80 Strand, London WC2R 0RL, England

First published in Puffin by Penguin Books India 2014

Text copyright © Arijit Ganguly 2014
Translation copyright © Aparna Chaudhuri 2014

All rights reserved

10 9 8 7 6 5 4 3 2 1

ISBN 9780143333012

Typeset in Minion by Eleven Arts, New Delhi
Printed at Replika Press Pvt. Ltd, India

Contents

Contents

Introduction

I have to say I was not one of those Bengali children who cut their milk teeth on the stories of Tenida. An avid and voracious reader growing up in Darjeeling, I preferred boys' adventure stories swiped from my elder brother's shelves to the soppier variants for girls which well-meaning but clueless relatives bought for me. Immersed as I was in the exciting (and invariably English language) world of *Commando* comics, *Sudden Apache Fighter*, *Biggles* and the *Three Investigators*, Potoldanga might well have been an undiscovered planet for all I knew (or cared). What a pleasure, then, to encounter Tenida's universe for the first time as an adult. In fact, I'd go so far as to say that this delayed pleasure has enabled me to relish it all the more—the extremely succulent 'Bengaliness' of the stories, their quaintness, and their humour. In Aparna Chaudhuri's crisp and crackling translation, Narayan Gangopadhyay's fiction comes alive for a whole new generation, who might find in Tenida an unlikely spokesman for many of the things that continue to plague them. Exams, for instance. A formidable serial failure in school exams, Tenida declaims to his gang—comprising Kyabla, Pelaram and Habul—'Examinations are all a conspiracy! A lot of donkeys learn their textbooks by heart and pass in a twinkling. It's failing that's difficult, you understand? Take me, for example. I go to the examination hall year after year, answer all the papers—but do I ever pass? I'm too much for any examiner. That's the real feat, see?'

Tenida is a champion *dhop-baaj* or puller of fast ones. He is also a master extortionist, despatching his chelas to buy treats which he devours with an appetite as gargantuan as his nose and as unabashed as his boastful behaviour. Consummate coward and grand connoisseur of freebies, there's nothing remotely glorious or admirable about him, and yet, riveting scamster that he is, he holds the gang of Potoldanga boys together as they fall in and out of all kinds of pickles. It's Kyabla who is the real brains of the gang (a lovely bit of wordplay, by the way, since Kyabla is one of those delightfully untranslatable Bengali words signifying anything from 'doofus' to 'dunce'), who salvages his boring best student status by displaying exemplary courage and powers of deduction, besides firing all manner of salvos at Tenida, slyly egging him on in the thick of combat just when he shows signs of turning tail. 'Why would you need guns?' he says to Tenida at one point, 'I hear each of your famous slaps topples a tommy-soldier on the Maidan. What would a hero like you want with guns?' It's Pelaram who is the narrator, sickly malarial Pela with a perpetually traumatized spleen, who, when he's not forced to sustain his feeble frame on catfish curry, is busy being distracted by wild berries and slapped by spooks. And last but not least, it's dear Habul with his Dhaka accent and his accommodating nature who manfully plays both nervous sidekick and generous contributor to the funds of the no-doubt pre-eminent Potoldanga Thunder Club.

For me the greatest reward was the wealth of culinary joshing between the boys. Perhaps this is a uniquely Bengali trait, this obsession with food metaphors (or do I just mean food?). Reading these stories made me hungry! For *jhalmuri* and samosas, chop-cutlets and chicken curry, *alu kabli* and *sheekh kabab*, thickly-buttered toast and *Mughlai parathas*—all those sinful things that adulthood warns against. But why should *you* resist? Dive right into this delicious book and let Tenida and the Potoldanga boys add some savoury-sweet zest to your life.

January 2014   Sampurna Chattarji

CHARMURTI
(The Four Heroes)

Uncle's Laughter

The school finals were over.

Our chat on the Chatterjees' front step was in full swing. There were the three of us—our president Tenida, Habul Sen and yours truly, Pelaram Banerjee. We live in Potoldanga and eat catfish stewed with the vegetable in question: *potol* or pointed gourd. Our fourth member, Kyabla, was yet to turn up.

All four of us had taken the exam. Kyabla's the best student—the headmaster has said he's going to get a scholarship. Habul Sen, native of Dhaka, son of East Bengal, will also make it to the first division. I've already tripped twice on the maths paper—this time, I might just manage third-division marks. And Tenida—

Well, the less said about him the better. He's sat for the Matriculation exam—and the Entrance, for all you know. This year it was the school finals: the Higher Secondary will probably be next. At school, he sits like a monument in Class Ten: no one can shift him an inch from his place.

Says the great man with a chuckle, 'Heh, heh, don't you understand? You need a couple of old-timers in the class, people who know the ropes. Who's to manage the new lot otherwise?'

I'd say the new boys were being quite well managed. Even Tenida's elder brother, the formidable Borda, whose voice sends us scurrying for cover, has been managed into mildness. Three or four years ago, he'd shake the house with his screams every time Tenida failed an exam, and do complex calculations to determine the exact amount of cow dung in his brother's head. Now he's given up as well. In fact, he's got so used to Tenida failing that if he suddenly manages to pass, Borda might just pass out altogether.

So there was nothing to disturb the peace of our adda.

True, our hapless Habul had once brought up the subject of examinations. But Tenida had wrinkled his nose disdainfully and said, 'That's enough! Examinations are all a conspiracy! A lot of donkeys learn their textbooks by heart and pass in a twinkling. It's failing that's difficult, you understand? Take me, for example. I go to the examination hall year after year, answer all the papers—but do I ever pass? I'm too much for any examiner. That's the real feat, see?'

'Absolutely,' I said. 'That's why I've been your follower these two years. Uncle's pulled my ears till they're each about a foot long, but I've got my toes dug into school all right.'

'Shut up,' scolded Tenida. 'I had great hopes for you once—thought you'd be a disciple after my own heart. But you've turned out to be the biggest traitor of them all. What made you get thirty-six whole marks on that maths paper? And when you did get them, why didn't you cross them out with a nice black line?'

I scratched my head and admitted I'd made a mistake.

'The world's against me,' sighed Tenida. 'Let it perish. But what shall we do now that the exams are over? Sit around twiddling our thumbs in Kolkata? It's no good if we don't go somewhere.'

'Yes, let's,' I agreed happily. 'There's my Ranga Pishima's house in Liluah. We can have some fun there for a few days . . .'

'Stop right there, Pela!' Tenida pulled a face. 'Long ears like a goat and a goat's brain to match. Liluah! That's the only place our genius can think of. Why not go to Hatibagan instead? Or to your own rooftop for some fresh air? I wish I'd never met your spotted spleen.'

'We could go somewhere else,' said a thoughtful voice with a strong Dhaka accent. 'What about Bardhaman? My uncle's the DSP of police there—'

'Boring old Bardhaman,' Tenida turned up his nose. 'There's no escaping the place if you're on a train. No matter where you're going it takes you through Bardhaman. It's all puffing engines and tooting horns—sounds as if they're celebrating the chariot festival on the platform. But then . . .' Tenida broke off to scratch the top of his head, 'you do get good sweets like *sitabhog* and *mihidana* there. Bardhaman's quite an idea, actually. It's a lot better than Liluah, at any rate.'

An insult to Ranga Pishima's noble name! I grew hot with indignation.

'It sounds all right,' I began. 'But the mosquitoes in Bardhaman are the size of small sparrows. Wait till a few sneak into your mosquito net. They'll make mihidana of you in a minute. And there's more . . .' I warmed to my theme . . . 'didn't Habul say his uncle's the DSP of police? Get into a fight, and you'll be in handcuffs before you know it.'

Tenida looked a little daunted. 'Rubbish!' he said weakly. 'What d'you say, Habul? What's this uncle of yours like?'

'Well, Pela isn't wrong,' admitted Habul after some thought. 'Uncle was in the army and he's got a temper to prove it.'

'That does it! No, East Bengal's addled your brain. Who wants to meddle with your military uncles? We're all right here—no need to go looking for trouble.'

Before the debate could progress further, Kyabla entered with a packet of *alu kabli* in his hand.

'There you are, Kyabla!' Tenida leapt to his feet and swooped down on the snack like a kite upon its prey. Having consumed half the bag in one gulp, he said approvingly, 'Excellent. Where did you buy it from?'

Surprisingly, Kyabla showed no sign of distress. He looked quite pleased, in fact. 'The man at the corner was selling it.'

'Is he still there? In that case, why don't you fetch another four annas' worth?'

'What's a bit of alu kabli?' said Kyabla dismissively. 'Why not pulao and chicken? Or prawn cutlets and pineapple chutney? Or sweet yoghurt and *rasagolla*?'

'No more!' begged Tenida. 'Don't even talk of such things. My stomach's rumbling already. If you talk like that, what's to save me from a heart attack?'

'You'll be the loser, then,' grinned Kyabla. 'They're all being cooked at our house tonight. My mother said I was to invite the three of you to dinner.'

We were stunned. A full three minutes passed in awed silence.

Then, leaping to his feet, Tenida demanded, 'Are you telling the truth, Kyabla? You're not joking?'

'Why should I be joking?' retorted Kabla. 'My uncle is visiting from Ranchi. He's the one who did all the shopping for dinner.'

'And the chicken? Are you sure there will be chicken? Look here, Kyabla, you can't disappoint a Brahmin when his hopes are high! Be careful—you'll be reborn as a chicken if you do.'

'Don't worry. There were half a dozen trussed-up chickens squawking in the courtyard when I left.'

'Trim–trim–tra–la–la–la—'

Tenida danced with joy. The three of us took up the chorus. A mongrel skulking down the alley yelped in shock, then tucked his tail between his legs and fled in the opposite direction.

The feast that night was beyond description. Watching Tenida eat, I was afraid he'd need a crane to lift him up once he'd finished. Not only did he polish off a couple of seers of meat and about a dozen cutlets, he seemed quite capable of eating the plate he was served on as well.

We met another entertaining person at the table—Kyabla's uncle. What stories he could tell! We laughed so much it hurt. On one shikaar, he had apparently spun a wild buffalo around by its tail. Another time, the branch he was perched on collapsed, dropping him on to a tiger's back. Far from gobbling him up, the tiger promptly keeled over unconscious. The poor beast probably thought it was being attacked by a ghost. In fact, it was still unconscious when they put it in a cage. Smelling salts and sprinkles of water finally brought it around.

We were listening to these stories after dinner on the roof of Kyabla's house. Ensconced in an armchair, Uncle smoked one cigarette after another and talked. We sat rapt on the rush mat at his feet. Uncle's bald pate glinted in the moonlight, and the red glow of his cigarette lit his face in an occasional unearthly flicker.

'So you want to go on a holiday?' he said. 'I can tell you of the perfect spot. You won't find another place as refreshing, or as pretty.'

'Ranchi?' asked Kyabla.

'No, no,' said Uncle. 'It's terribly hot there now. And so crowded—no, Ranchi's no good.'

'Darjeeling or Shillong?' guessed Tenida.

'Too cold,' countered Uncle. 'It's painful to be roasted, but I don't see much point in freezing either. Not any of those places.'

It was my turn to contribute. Bereft of inspiration, I blurted out, 'Gobordanga, then?'

'Shut up, Pela, shut up, I say!' Tenida bared his teeth at me. 'Oaf that you are, what place would you think of that wasn't Gobordanga or Liluah?'

'Stop, stop,' interposed Uncle. 'Most people in Kolkata haven't even heard of the place I'm talking about. It's not far from Ranchi. You can get there from Hazaribagh or Ramgarh. Once you get off the bus, it's about three miles by bullock cart. It's a lovely spot, all rippling blue lakes and thick forests of sal and mahua. You'll see deer by day, and plenty of rabbits and junglefowl. There's a Santhal settlement close by, so you'll get cheap milk and meat. Fish from the lake is a couple of paise per seer. I've bought a bungalow on top of a hillock. It's a splendid place, built by an Englishman. The view from the verandah stretches for miles, and the little waterfall beside it never runs dry. Go and spend a month there. You skinny lads will come back as lusty as the heroes of yore.'

Tenida's colossal dinner had left him slumped against a cushion. Now excitement made him sit up straight.

'We'll go, all four!'

Uncle lit another cigarette. 'Excellent idea, but there's a hitch.'

'What?'

'The house has some problems.'

'What problems?'

'Well, the local Santhals say it's haunted. Spooks get up to all kinds of mischief every now and then. You hear footsteps, bumps and bangs, unearthly screams—yet there isn't a soul to be seen. I'll admit that I've only been to the place about three times since I bought it, and each time I arrived in the morning and left at dusk. So I've never been bothered by these nocturnal noises. But I'm wondering if you're brave enough to stay there.'

'Pooh!' said Tenida stoutly. 'All rubbish! There are no such things as ghosts, Uncle. Of course we'll stay. If we do meet any spooks, we won't come back to Kolkata without driving them into the lunatic asylum at Ranchi. And—'

But Tenida's sentence remained unfinished. Stopping short, he flung both his arms around Habul Sen.

'Let me go!' protested Habul in alarm. 'You'll make my stomach burst!'

But Tenida only clutched him tighter and stammered, 'What . . . what's that . . . what's that on the roof?'

A black cloud had obscured the moon. An eerie darkness lay thick about us. On the roof next to ours, a pair of unearthly eyes glowed brightly through the gloom.

And that instant, Kyabla's uncle let out a thunderous laugh. My ears rang with the sound, my sickly spleen went knocking around my innards, and the chicken I had eaten seemed about to burst cackling out of my stomach.

Never in my life had I heard such deafening, diabolical laughter.

The Pot of Holy Snakes

What with Uncle's manic laughter and those incandescent eyes shining at us from that rooftop, I was prepared to shout 'Praise to Mother Kali!' and run for the stairs. But then we heard a plaintive *miaow, miaow, miaow* . . .

The owner of the fiery eyes leapt gracefully to the parapet, and then on to the cornice of a neighbouring house.

Uncle stopped laughing for a minute to remark, 'A tomcat makes you scream, and you want to stay in that *dak* bungalow!' With another nasal chuckle, he added, 'Heroes don't grow on every tree, after all!'

Kyabla was the only one of us to have remained relatively unmoved—the cheek of that boy! 'No, but like potted plants in Potoldanga!' he put in.

'Or like yams in the yard!' gasped Habul, wriggling out of Tenida's stranglehold.

It was my turn now. 'Or on the ground like groundnuts!'

Tenida had been getting his breath back all this while. Now he bared his teeth and hissed, 'Shut up, all of you. That's enough nonsense. Really, Uncle, we weren't scared at all. Pela here is such a coward that we thought we'd play a prank on him.'

What fun! Blame it on me, as usual. I assumed the aggrieved expression that makes me look like a bad-tempered billygoat. 'No, Uncle, I wasn't afraid. But I could see Tenida trembling, so I shouted to reassure him.'

'Reassure me? My young hero!' Screwing up his nose and looking as peeved as a piece of mango pulp, Tenida turned on me, 'Look here, Pela, any more smart talk from you and I'll give your ears a year's worth of twisting.'

'Stop, that's enough,' Uncle broke in. 'You gentlemen are obviously bravehearts of the first order. But let's return to the point. Do you really want to go to Jhantipahari?'

'Jhantipahari? Where on earth is that? Good God, who'd want to go rot there?' exclaimed Tenida.

'How very odd! Didn't you want to go there just a minute ago?' replied Uncle.

'Oh, did we?' Tenida scratched his head doubtfully. 'I didn't realize. But you see, Jhantipahari . . . well, rather a strange name for a place, isn't it?'

'Grotesque,' agreed Habul.

'Sounds exactly the spot for a spook,' said I.

'So you won't go, after all,' said Uncle with another nasal cackle. 'Scared, are you?'

Now Tenida bounced up. 'Scared?' he exclaimed, doing a

quick push-up. 'I don't know the name of fear!' Thumping himself on the chest, he declared in Hindi, 'I'll go! I'll go alone!'

'And what if the spooks come after you?' prodded Kyabla.

'Then I'll make chutney of them!' High on a heady draught of courage, Tenida declared, 'I'll go alone if no one else wants to come!'

I felt a sudden surge of enthusiasm. 'I'll go!'

'So will I,' volunteered Kyabla.

'I'm with you,' Dhaka tones struck in.

'You won't be frightened?' enquired Uncle.

'Not at all,' Tenida puffed out his chest.

I was about to say something similar when that rascal Kyabla interrupted. 'Of course, there's no telling what might happen if you run into a tomcat after sunset.'

Uncle let out another ear-splitting peal of laughter. Tenida bellowed, 'Look, Kyabla, any more such talk and I'll punch your nose till—'

'Till it "knows" better,' I supplied.

'Exactly. You've hit the nail on the head.' Tenida's approving thump on my back made me yell.

I won't go into everything that followed. How your four heroes persuaded their families to agree to their holiday is a tale that would make another Mahabharata. Best save those details for a different story. The important thing is that three days later, with suitcases hoisted on our shoulders and bedrolls tucked under our arms, we met at Howrah station.

The train was almost empty. Who'd be crazy enough to go to Ranchi in summer? Finding an inter-class compartment going begging, we took possession of it and laid out four beds. I was about to make myself comfortable on one when Tenida called out, 'Pela!'

'What is it now?'

'I'm famished, pal. Feel as if a team of moles are holding a boxing match in my belly.'

'What?' I exclaimed. 'Didn't you eat about thirty *luchis* and a seer of mutton curry just before you left home? Where's it all gone?'

'Got one of those all-devouring worms in your stomach, have you?' suggested Habul.

'Nothing less,' agreed Tenida. 'You're absolutely right. Anything that goes in is swallowed by flames and reduced to ashes.' He laughed in a lordly manner. 'After all, I'm a Brahmin's son, Sage Agastya's direct descendant! If the ogre Vatapi entered my stomach, I'd digest him straight away. That's what you call holy fire.'

'You a Brahmin!' snorted Kyabla. 'Do you wear a sacred thread?'

'A sacred thread?' Tenida gulped. 'Well, you see, it's such a nuisance in summer, snaps every time you scratch your back. And why would a true Brahmin need a sacred thread? Holy fire is quite enough. But honestly, what should we do? Those moles are playing a regular game of kabbadi in my stomach!'

'How can it be helped?' said Kyabla. 'Why don't you referee the match?'

'What did you say, Kyabla?'

'Who, me? Nothing, nothing at all!' Kyabla flattened himself out on his bunk.

Habul Sen chose this moment to say: 'Punch those guts and sit tight.'

'Whose guts should I punch? Yours?' Fist raised, Tenida was about to come over and investigate.

'Not mine, not mine . . . Pela's,' said Habul quickly.

Wonderful! Why should my guts have all the bad luck? Leaping nimbly on to a bunk, I protested, 'Why me? Why should my stomach swallow your punches? It doesn't need them!'

'If you don't buy me something to swallow this minute, you'll swallow a few of my best punches,' threatened Tenida. 'Look at all those vendors passing—can't you call one? *Puri-kachori,* oranges, chocolate, *dalmoot . . .'*

'All I can see is a bootblack. Will he do?' I asked innocently.

'That's it—' Tenida looked ready to pounce on me. I was thinking of jumping through the window when the bell rang noisily. The engine trumpeted, and the train began to move.

The door suddenly swung open. A gentleman entered the compartment with a large and suspicious-looking clay pot in his hand. At the same moment, someone on the platform hurled something through the window. It landed neatly and heavily on the back of Tenida's neck. Tenida yelped.

But just as he was about to glare at the offender and demand 'What d'you think you're doing, mister?' something seemed to strike him dumb. Not just him but all of us.

The new arrival was a vision to behold. A sadhu of truly awe-inspiring proportions! His head was all bushy hair and his face a riot of whiskers. Fat *rudraksha* beads hung around his neck, a *tilak* of bright red vermilion marked his forehead and his feet were encased in *nagra* shoes with upturned toes.

Putting down his mysterious pot, the sadhu addressed us. 'Don't worry, my son, that is only my bedding. My disciple threw it through the window in his haste. I hope you are not badly hurt?'

'No—not much, Baba. I only hope I feel better in a week.' Tenida began massaging his neck. But the holy man had my full approval. Tenida had been about to punch me in the stomach—look at him now!

The sadhu now smiled and answered, 'Felled by the blow of a bed, my son? An entire kabuliwallah, complete with a half-tonne sack of asafoetida, once fell from his bunk and landed on my shoulder. But did it kill me? I recovered after just a week at the hospital. That's what you call yogic power.'

'Really? Then you're a great man, sir. Let me take the dust of your venerable feet.' Tenida performed a swift pranaam.

'Excellent,' approved the sadhu. 'May you be blessed with good sense. Now, who are you, boys? And where are you off to?

'Baba, we're going to Ramgarh for a holiday. My name is Teni . . . I mean Bhajahari Mukherjee. This is Pelaram Banerjee, who's always running a fever and has a monstrous spleen in his stomach. This is Habul Sen—he might be from Dhaka but he contributes generously to the funds of our Potoldanga Thunder Club. And that's Kyabla Mitra—he always comes first in class and treats us to feasts of pulao and chicken at his house.'

'Pulao and chicken!' Deep in his beard, the holy man seemed to control his watering mouth with difficulty. 'Excellent, excellent!'

'Baba, which of the great saints are you?' Habul asked over piously folded hands.

'My name? The Great Gloomyswami.'

'Gloomyswami? Good God!' muttered Kyabla audibly.

'Awed by this, son Kyabla? Do you know what my guru's name was? Reverberatingdrumaswami. His guru's name was Hot-sun-and-poached-cock's-egg-with-jam-aswami; his guru was called—'

'No more, O Great Gloomyswami—I'm short of breath already! It'll be a heart attack next!' Flat on my bunk, I had to beg for mercy.

The Great Gloomyswami smiled pityingly. 'Only a boy! Well, you can't be blamed. After the holy name of the guru fourth above my own was vouchsafed to me, I hiccupped for two whole days. Let it be. I can see there are four of you, and all bound for Ramgarh. I alight at Muri, to go on to Ranchi. Well, my sons, my yogic slumber is profound and not easily broken. The train reaches Muri at dawn. It would be a great service if you'd wake me up.'

'Don't you worry, Baba. We'll wake you up at Ghatshila.'

'No, no, my son, no need to wake me quite so early. We reach Ghatshila at midnight.'

'Tatanagar then?'

'That too is in the small hours, my son. Calm down. To wake me at Muri will be quite sufficient.'

'All right, we will,' promised Tenida. 'You can sink into your yogic slumber quite safely now, Baba.'

'I can indeed,' agreed the holy man. 'But where?' he continued, looking around the compartment. 'You four boys have taken the four lower berths. I'm a holy man. Upper bunks disturb my yogic repose.'

'Why should you sleep on an upper bunk, Master?' responded Tenida instantly. 'Pela will sleep above, he loves upper berths!'

What villainy! Upper berths have always given me the shudders—I keep feeling as if I'll fall out. And here was Tenida saying—

'Certainly not,' I declared. 'I hate sleeping on upper bunks!'

Tenida glared at me. 'Look here, Pela—none of your tricks around holy men, or you'll go to hell for sure. Master, please shove Pela's bedding off the bunk, he'll sleep wherever he likes.'

'Ah, may you live long.' With that pious sentiment, the sadhu heaved my bedding on to the berth above and spread his own out below. I looked on mutinously.

Just before getting into bed, the sadhu tucked the mysterious pot under his berth. Tenida had been eyeing it for a while. Now he asked, 'What's in the pot, Master?'

The Great Gloomyswami gave a start. 'In the pot! In that pot are the most terrible creatures, my son! Holy snakes!'

'Holy snakes?' exclaimed Habul. 'What are they, Master?'

Gloomyswami rolled his eyes alarmingly. 'Oh, it's an awesome miracle! They're terribly poisonous snakes, but I've tamed them with the power of my spells. They live on a soothing diet of milk and bananas and take the name of the Lord.'

'Snakes that take the name of the Lord!' I exclaimed involuntarily.

'You can do anything with yogic power.' The Great Gloomyswami laughed. 'But don't any of you go near that pot. They'll bite you in a jiffy unless you know the right charms. Take care!'

'Yes sir, we'll be very careful,' promised Tenida meekly.

The holy man peered at us suspiciously. 'Yes, very careful!' he repeated. 'Don't even look at it by mistake! Well, now can I go to sleep in peace?'

'By all means.'

It didn't even take five minutes. The Great Gloomyswami's snores began to sound in regular rhythm.

The train rocked me to sleep before I knew it. But I was rudely poked awake. Tenida was tickling my ribs.

'Come on down, you donkey! Once the sadhu baba wakes up you won't get anything!'

I looked. The pot of holy snakes sat on Tenida's berth. Kabla and Habul Sen had taken off the lid and were rapidly devouring the contents: rasagollas and dark fat balls of *ledikenis*.

Tenida hissed at me again, 'What are you gaping at? Get down, quick! The pot of holy snakes will need its mouth tied up again once we've finished with it!'

I needed no more urging. A single bound and I was on the floor; with a swipe of my paw I had scooped up two ledikenis.

'Hold on, hold on!' Tenida warned. 'Don't finish the lot! Leave me a couple!'

Leaving Tatanagar behind, the train leapt into the darkness once more. But the Great Gloomyswami's snores never stopped sounding in rhythmic grunts and whirrs.

Given the way we had pounced on that pot, it didn't take us more than five minutes to scrape it clean. More than half fell to Tenida's share. Habul Sen and I took care of the rest. Only Kyabla, being the youngest, couldn't put up much of a fight. After a couple of ledikenis, he fell to licking his fingers.

But Tenida was still loath to relinquish the pot. In the end, he tilted it over his lips and drank even the last drops of syrup. Then, screwing up his nose, he complained, 'Blast, I think I've swallowed a few of those big black ants now. Live ones, too. They won't start biting my insides, will they?'

'They might,' said Habul solemnly.

21

'Let them, it's all one to me! Didn't I swallow a hornet with a hog plum once? If that didn't hurt me, what damage can a few ants do?'

'Oh, you can swallow the Sunderbans with all the tigers in them. What's to stop you?' Kyabla gave up licking his fingers and heaved a deep sigh.

The Great Gloomyswami's snores had continued unabated through this exchange. Snores fortified by yogic strength were a different thing altogether!

'Grunt on, but your sweets are gone,' Tenida addressed him. 'Think you're clever, don't you? Clobbering me with that great bedroll! My shoulder's still throbbing. Well, we've had our revenge. What d'you say, Pela?'

'Vengeance is ours,' I agreed.

The empty pot of holy snakes had its mouth securely retied by Tenida. Then he flopped on to his bunk and said, 'Come on, let's get some sleep. The fire in my belly's died a little.'

Habul and I were equally satisfied on that point. Only Kyabla continued to grumble, 'Ate everything, the lot of you. What about me?'

'That's enough, don't talk so much,' admonished Tenida. 'A little kid like you—won't you be ill if you eat too much? Go on, go to sleep—'

I don't know if Kyabla took his advice, but Tenida himself was asleep in less than two minutes. His nose answered the Swamiji's grunt for grunt. I don't know how long their dialogue lasted. Trying to keep the flies off my face, I fell asleep, too.

The Banana Skin

'Muri! Muri Junction!'

I sat up with a start and saw pale morning light outside. Kyabla was awake, and nursing a cup of tea. Habul Sen yawned a couple of times and peered blearily at the Baba without getting up. But the holy man's nose was still blaring like a foghorn. Tenida's was blaring in response, as if to say, 'The pot's empty.'

Kyabla poked Tenida sharply in the ribs.

'Hey, hey! Who's that tickling me?' Tenida sat up indignantly.

'The train's been standing at Muri station for almost ten minutes now. Aren't you going to wake Swamiji up?'

Tenida looked first at the pot, then at its owner. 'How long before the train leaves?' he asked.

'It'll pull out any minute now, I think.'

'Let it start. We'll wake him once the train's begun to move. If he gets up now and finds his precious pot empty,

23

there'll be hell to pay! He's built like an ox. With the rasagollas gone, he'll eat us instead. Better we—'

Before Tenida could finish, a mighty bellow was heard outside: 'O Master, in which of the compartments are you enjoying your yogic repose?'

It was no mere shout, the voice sounded like a clap of thunder. The whole station shook. The Great Gloomyswami sat up with a start.

'Wake up, my Lord! The train's about to pull out—'

'Why, that's my disciple Gajeswar!' The holy man thrust his head out of the window. 'Gaja—son Gajeswar! Here I am!'

The door of the compartment burst open to admit a man whose proportions made me leap promptly on to my bunk. Tenida and Habul hastily lay down again. Kyabla alone could do nothing—the cup of tea in his hand simply dropped to the floor with a clang.

'Ooh, I've had it—my foot's scalded!' yelled the Swami. 'Are these lads dolts? I told them to wake me at Muri, and see what they've done! A little longer and I'd have been carried over.'

Gajeswar cast a glance in our direction. That one glare was enough to turn my blood to water. The massive Swami looked a mere stick beside him. Gajeswar's skin was as black as the bottom of a pot, his body the size of an elephant. A yard-long pigtail hung from his shaven head. Eyeing us grimly, he said, 'Boys these days are all the same, Master—as if they've been imported direct from Kishkinda! With your permission, I'll just box each of their ears.'

A clip on the ear from Gajeswar was all we needed. Our ears would probably come off in his hands. We shrank like sugar balls in syrup. But we were in luck—just that minute, the bell jangled for the train to move.

Gajeswar began bustling about. 'Get off, get off, Master! The train's about to leave. We'll let their ears off for now. Time enough for that later. Now get off, get off—'

So saying, Gajeswar almost hoisted the swami on to his shoulder with his boxes and bedroll and bore him off the train. At the same moment, the whistle blew and the train began to move.

We were still sitting frozen with fear. Gajeswar's giant arm, so like an elephant's trunk, swam before our eyes. A great danger had passed us by.

But the train had barely moved an arm's length when Swamiji set up a frantic outcry. 'My pot! My pot of rasagollas!'

Tenida immediately held the pot aloft. 'You're mistaken, Master, not rasagollas but holy snakes! Here—'

He flung the pot out on to the platform.

'Oh dear, oh dear . . .' The swami began to run towards it, then stood stock-still. The pot lay in fragments on the floor. But there wasn't half a rasagolla to be seen, nor a morsel of ledikeni.

'Baba, your snakes have escaped,' I yelled. 'No need to worry now!'

25

But what was this? Gajeswar was pounding towards the train like a charging elephant. His piercing eyes seemed to be shooting fire. He was running fit to beat the train. Any moment now, he'd leap into the compartment!

I was about to clamber up on to my bunk again and Tenida was making for the bathroom, when—O gift of God!—a banana skin!

Gajeswar's foot skidded and he fell flat on the platform. It was no ordinary slip, more like a second Fall of Man. *Khoya* spattered around him like a hail of bullets.

'That's done it!' a clamour rose from the platform. But Gajeswar wasn't doing anything. He lay motionless for five seconds, then hobbled to his feet.

'Saved by a banana skin!' we heard his distant, despairing howl.

The train was travelling at full speed now. Tenida drew a deep breath. 'God is great.'

Jhanturam of Jhantipahari

The rest of the journey proved fairly uneventful. There was a lot of laughter over Gajeswar's accident. What a crash he'd fallen with—just like the giant Ghatotkacha in the Mahabharata! Of course, the thought of him falling on us was a different matter altogether.

'Another minute, and he'd have been on the train,' remarked Habul. 'And beaten us into jelly.'

Tenida screwed up his nose. '"Beaten us into jelly!"' he mimicked. 'Easier said than done! It's Teni Mukherjee of Potoldanga you've got here—one ju-jitsu twist and Muri or no Muri, our friend would have been no more than a handful of *muri*, just puffed rice! Or flattened like rice flakes.'

Kyabla giggled.

'You laughing, Kyabla?'

Kyabla's a sly bird. He replied immediately, 'It wasn't me, it was Pela'.

'Pela!'

Why on earth would I laugh? A severe pain had been gnawing at my stomach for quite a while now, brought on by the contents of the pot of holy snakes. For all I knew, I might have swallowed a few black ants as well. Wearing an injured expression, I protested, 'Why should I laugh? What's so funny?'

'I'm warning you, Pela, mind my words,' growled Tenida. 'Laugh again for no reason, and I'll uproot those radishes you call molars. Blast—that Gajeswar got off too easy! If he'd just caught up with us, he'd have known the terror of a Potoldanga twist. If we ever run into him again . . .'

Little did we know that we would. And I, Pelaram of Potoldanga, would have been happier if we hadn't.

A little later, the train stopped at Ramgarh.

Kyabla's uncle had advised us to find a bullock cart. But city boys on a bullock cart—that would be absurd!

'It's only six miles,' said Tenida confidently. 'Let's walk it.'

'By all means,' I agreed. 'Singing birds and shady trees . . .'

'The scent of flowers and a southerly breeze,' continued Kyabla.

'And wayside trees with ripe jackfruits and mangoes dangling from them,' Tenida added.

'Not to mention their owners charging at us with sticks,' pointed out Habul.

'Blast, ruined it completely!' exclaimed Tenida in annoyance. 'We were talking about mangoes and jackfruits, and he drags in sticks and stones! That's why I don't feel like going anywhere with you soulless lot. Now come on, quick march.'

Shouldering our suitcases and bedrolls, we set off.

We soon found out, however, that evening strolls on the Maidan and trudging six miles with boxes and bedding weren't quite the same thing. We had scarcely covered half a mile when my malaria-ridden spleen began to throb in complaint.

'Tenida, what about a little rest?'

Tenida readily agreed.

'Not a bad idea. And my appetite feels quite lively again. What about a bit of refreshment, eh, Kyabla?' So saying, he glanced at Kyabla's suitcase. He had already noted that it contained a brand new tin of biscuits.

Kyabla immediately clasped the suitcase under his arm.

'What d'you mean by refreshment? You just ate eight samosas at Ramgarh station!'

'What if I did?' Tenida yanked away Kyabla's suitcase with a single tug. 'Do you expect me to walk six miles on them? I've got a better appetite than that!'

He sat down heavily under a tree and opened the case. There was no lock on it—the tin was out in a trice.

It was crammed with crisp cream cracker biscuits. What could we do but sit down as well? Tenida devoured most of them—a few fell to our share. Only Kyabla ate nothing but sat looking on with a face like the black end of a pot.

It was no joke, that six-mile tramp. Habul had reserved two loaves of bread, which vanished next. But Tenida's hunger refused to be appeased. He had only to see a wayside shop selling puffed rice and rice flakes to flop down and command, 'Now then, Pela, fork out a couple of annas, my stomach's churning with hunger.'

Four miles on, the road became a winding mountain trail. Paths of red soil looped through dense sal forests. We hadn't gone very far when we began to get the creeps.

'O Tenida, there are tigers in forests like these,' Kyabla pointed out.

Tenida's face grew pale. 'What rubbish!'

'Bears as well, I've heard,' added Habul.

'Hmmm,' said Tenida.

I couldn't remember what came after bears and tigers. 'And probably a hippopotamus or two,' I ventured.

Tenida bared his teeth at me. 'Shut up, Pela. Do you think I'm an idiot? A hippopotamus is a water horse! What would it be doing in a forest?'

'Well, what if there are spooks?' I suggested.

'Spook yourself!' retorted Tenida angrily. 'Why should there be ghosts here? There isn't a living soul in the place. Whom would they spook?'

'Well, what if they come along to wring our necks?' countered Kyabla swiftly. 'You're our leader . . . what if they like your neck best of all?'

Tenida shot out a hand to grab Kyabla's ear. Kyabla sidestepped smartly. And Tenida's foot came down on a fresh pat of cow dung.

Crash! Thud! A fall to beat Gajeswar's!

I was almost clapping my hands in glee when suddenly—

A six-foot-tall apparition loomed against the trees—reed-thin, wild-haired, dark-skinned. A ghastly grin split the uncouth features. Speak of a spook and it comes straight out of the forest!

I was the first to break into a run, calling on my ancestors for rescue. Kyabla leapt into the nearest tree. Tenida tried to follow him but skidded on the cow dung again. Habul Sen clapped his hands over his eyes and began to scream, 'Ghosts, ghosts! Ram, Ram!'

The phantom figure laughed thunderously.

'Young sirs, you're scaring yourselves for no reason! I am Jhanturam of Jhantipahari. I got Babu's letter and came ahead to meet you. No need to be frightened, no need to be frightened!'

By this time, I was almost half a mile away. Kyabla was clinging to the crown of the tree. Habul was chanting energetically, 'Spooks are my kin/ They'll do me no sin'. Tenida was sitting stock-still in the cow dung. For all I knew, he'd lost his senses from shock.

The spectre reassured us, 'Nothing to be scared of, young masters, nothing to be scared of! I'm Jhanturam of Jhantipahari, your servant!'

The Mysterious Footsteps

What a nuisance! Without being a spook, the wretch had managed to spook us thoroughly. My heart refused to stop pounding for a good half hour. Tenida stood up, covered in cow dung. Scratching his legs madly where monster tree-ants had attacked him, Kyabla climbed down. Habul's knees kept knocking together. And after that brisk half-mile run, my sickly spleen felt as if it'd burst out of my stomach.

Tenida was the first to pull himself together.

'Jhanturam?' He ground his teeth. 'Well, why d'you look like a ghoul?'

'What can I do, Khokababu, it's how God made me.'

'How God made you? Poppycock!' Tenida pulled a face. 'As if God didn't have better things to do! God never made you—ghouls did, understand?'

'Aye.' Jhanturam didn't seem to mind.

Now Kyabla came forward. 'Well then, why were you lurking behind that bush?'

Jhanturam smiled apologetically through a mouthful of crooked teeth. 'What could I do, Dadababu? I had set out for the station. On the way, I felt so sleepy that I thought I'd take a nap. I'd fallen fast asleep, but a few mosquitoes crawled into my nose. Waking up, I saw you coming. I was going to meet you when you got into a panic and made such a to-do.' He snickered sinisterly.

'That's enough!' scolded Kyabla. 'You can stop laughing now. Call those teeth? They look like a row of radishes. Now come on, quick, show us the way to Jhantipahari.'

Truly, Jhantipahari was a splendid place.

Grotesque as the name might sound, you had only to set foot here to feel soothed. Hills alight with palash and sal woods rose on three sides, the blooming palash glowing like red fire. A hundred different kinds of birds flew about, like streaks of colour in the sky. The bungalow faced a lake of rippling blue water edged by gently trembling *kalmi* vines, into which fishing cormorants, sinuous-necked as cobras, dipped quickly every now and then.

Uncle's bungalow stood on a little hillock close to the lake, surrounded by woods on three sides. Built of red brick, it had green doors and windows and a roof of red tiles. Coming upon it suddenly, you'd think it was another cluster of palash flowers, with a green leaf or two peeping out amidst the red.

Such a lovely place, such sweet fresh air, such a picturesque house, and rumours of haunting? Good lord, it just wasn't possible.

The rooms in the bungalow were splendidly furnished. There were tables, chairs, deckchairs, mirrors, clothes horses and everything else you could think of. Plump mattresses lay on the bedsteads. No sooner had we reached than Jhantu made up four inviting beds in two rooms. We sat down comfortably in cane chairs on the verandah. Jhanturam brought us omelettes and tea. Then he enquired, 'Would the young sirs like fish or chicken for lunch?'

'Chicken! Chicken!' we clamoured in chorus.

Tenida sucked down the water flooding his mouth. 'And hurry up, will you? It's noon already . . . feels as if the fire of Creation's raging in my insides. I warn you I'll start eating the chairs and tables if you take too long.'

'You'd be quite capable of it,' muttered a voice with a Dhaka accent.

'What was that you said, Habul?'

'Nothing, nothing!' Habul hastily covered his tracks. 'Just that I'm sure Jhantu can cook very quickly.'

Jhanturam went off. 'What if he does look frightful?' mused Tenida. 'He's a good man, that Jhanturam.'

'Hospitable chap,' I agreed. 'If he cooks us chicken curry every day, we'll be pink within a week.'

Tenida glared at me. 'Much good it'll do you! You're frail from malaria and chock-full of pills. Our fare won't suit you. From tomorrow, I'm putting you on a diet. Weak curry of raw plantains and *gandal* leaves. Can't have you perish in a strange place . . . who'll handle the fuss?'

'You needn't worry about that,' I said peevishly. 'I'm

through with that curry of gandal leaves. If I die, it'll be with chicken inside me.'

'To be reborn as one in your next life. Cock-a-doodle-doo!' yodelled that idiot Kyabla in a sudden fit of mirth. I sat scratching my nose angrily.

It was two by the time we sat down to lunch. Ah, it wasn't chicken curry that Jhantu had cooked—it tasted like an infusion of nectar and made us feel warm and sleepy. After that tiring night on the train, we were asleep as soon as our heads touched the soft pillows.

When Jhanturam came to wake us with our evening tea, the sun was sinking behind the mountains. The woods of sal and palash were dark masses against the hills, and the water of the lake was slate grey. The afternoon had spread around us in exhilarating beauty. Now everything lay under an eerie pall. The whirr of crickets beat loudly from the bushes, and rose from the woods behind the bungalow.

We had planned to explore the banks of the lake that evening, but strange shivers ran up and down our spines. We remembered Kolkata, where evening lights would be shining in windows, crowds gathering before the cinemas. Here in Jhantipahari, it was only the dusk that gathered and thickened as the crickets screamed louder, and a sort of stifled terror grew great around us.

Sitting on the verandah, we tried to strike up a conversation, but it lacked the usual spirit. Jhanturam had left a burning lantern in front of us. Around it, the darkness looked positively black.

At last, Tenida suggested, 'Come on, let's sing.'
'Not a bad idea,' said Kyabla. He set up a screech—

We will cleanse your stains of shame, Ma,
Redeem our human name, Ma . . .

No more was needed. The three of us joined in lustily. What a song it was!

All of our voices sound like slates being scraped. Tenida's, in particular, surpasses description. The story goes that he had once taken up a *kirtan* with such zest that the Chatterjee's pet cuckoo died of a heart attack. Now we set up such a rousing refrain that it brought an astonished Jhanturam running out to see what was wrong.

Perhaps we had all been struck by the same brilliant thought. Even if Jhantipahari was really haunted, no ghost could stand our song for long. They'd run for the hills before they were much older.

But the night proved us wrong.

Kyabla and I were sharing a bedroom, and Tenida and Habul the one next to it. A lantern winked dimly in the room: chairs, tables and mirrors all stood around looking rather strange in its unsteady light. Fear clamped down on my heart. For a long time I lay tossing and turning. Listening intently for noises, I could hear only the seven notes of Tenida's octave-spanning snores. Through the glass window I could see the dark heads of the mountains, brilliant with clustered stars. I don't know when I fell asleep.

Suddenly, click—click—clop—click—

I woke up with a start. Someone was walking about.
But where?

In this very room. It was the noise of booted feet.

Stretching out a hand, I turned up the flame of the lantern. No, there was no intruder in the room. But the footsteps were as loud as before. Someone was walking around—no doubt about that! Click, click, clop, clop—

'Kyabla!' I shrieked.

Kyabla leapt up. 'What? What's the matter?'

'Someone's walking around the room!'

Kyabla's spirit of enquiry left me stunned. He was out of bed in an instant. And in another second, a little mouse had scuttled through a hole in the door frame and vanished into the outer darkness.

Kyabla laughed aloud.

'What a coward you are, Pela! That mouse had got into an old torn shoe and was dancing about. That's what made all the noise. Was that what scared you?'

I rose hotly to the bait. 'Ho, d'you think I was really scared? Forget mice, even if a Brahmin's ghost were to arrive this minute—'

But the boast died on my lips. A long shriek pierced the still air. It was no human scream. A burst of unearthly laughter followed, laughter that sounded as if it had issued from the pits of hell to shake this frail bungalow of Jhantipahari to its foundations.

An Eventful Night

Long after that blood-curdling laugh had died away, it seemed as if the Jhantipahari dak bungalow was still quivering with terror. I had dived for the safety of my sheets. Even the gallant Kyabla had leapt back into his bed. My hands and feet were as cold as ice and my teeth were chattering loudly. From what I could make out, Kyabla wasn't in great form either.

Nearly ten minutes passed.

Kyabla was the first to recover his courage. In rather hollow tones, he asked, 'What d'you think the game is, Pela?'

'G-g-ghosts!' I quavered from under my sheet.

Kyabla had sat up in bed. I watched him, peering out cautiously from the shelter of my bedclothes.

'The question is,' he mused, 'why would ghosts want to laugh here in the first place?'

'Where would they laugh but in a haunted house? Even a ghost needs a place to laugh in,' I tried to argue.

Kyabla scratched his head thoughtfully. 'But why in this way, in the middle of the night? What's the point of waking us with that frightful din?'

'Midnight's the right time for ghosts,' I pointed out. 'D'you expect to find them giggling in College Square at midday?'

'That's what they should do,' insisted Kyabla. 'At least we'd be able to settle things face to face. But no, they'll practise their ha-ha declensions at the oddest of times. Ha-ha-ho-ho-hah-hah. Tell me, Pela, what makes ghosts laugh that creepy laughter so often?'

'How would I know?' I retorted, annoyed. 'Why don't you find a ghost and ask?'

Kyabla quietly got out of bed again. 'Let's do that, Pela,' he said. 'Let's see for ourselves what these ghosts look like. We'll tell them that the sons of four respectable men happen to be staying in this house at the moment. To disturb them with this ghastly cackle at this time of night is a serious offence.'

What was Kyabla saying? My hair stood on end with horror.

'Are you out of your mind?'

'Why should I be?' Our Kyabla was a spunky kid. Smiling a little, he said, 'D'you know what I think? I think ghosts are scared of people, too.'

'Scared? What are you talking about?'

'What else? Why d'you think there aren't any spooks in Kolkata? Why can't you catch a glimpse of a ghost's pigtail

39

in the daytime? Why are these ones cackling outside? Don't they have the courage to come in?'

'Ram, Ram!' I exclaimed. 'Don't even utter those words, Kyabla! Wasn't what you heard of their laughter enough? Any moment now, a couple of bodiless heads might start dancing about the room!'

A dangerous young sinner, this Kyabla! He replied at once, 'By all means! I've never seen a dance of bodiless heads—it sounds like fun! All right, I'll count to three. If these ghosts have any courage at all, they'll appear in this room and start dancing around it before I finish. It's a challenge, spooks! One, two ...'

What a disaster! What was wrong with Kyabla? Was he making fun of ghosts? Why, they can even read your thoughts! I cowered under my blanket. They'd be here in a trice now. Any moment and—

'Three!' announced Kyabla.

I lay stock-still under the bedclothes, rigid as marble, incapable of the least turn or twitch. Something horrible was sure to happen now. The ghosts were coming ... they were coming ... here they were ...

But nothing happened. The ghosts had probably decided that a pipsqueak like Kyabla was beneath their notice.

Kyabla crowed, 'There, you see! I challenged them, but were they brave enough to respond? Come on, let's try something different. Tenida and Habul must be up by now. Let's go meet these spooks, all four of us.'

I was breathless from fear.

'Kyabla, you'll get yourself killed for certain.'

Kyabla wasn't listening. Crossing over to my bed, he grabbed my hand. 'Get up!'

Gripping the sheet, I clung desperately to the mattress.

'Have you gone crazy, Kyabla? Go back to sleep!'

But Kyabla persisted. He really seemed possessed by some inner demon. 'Get up, I tell you!' he commanded, tugging at me unmercifully. 'Are we to sit tight and let these wretched ghosts ruin our sleep? Not a chance! Get up, quick!'

So saying, he began yanking at me so violently that I landed on the floor with a bump, sheets and all.

'Hey Kyabla, what d'you think you're doing?'

Would Kyabla listen? With another almighty tug, he pulled me to my feet. 'Come on, let's see if Tenida and Habul are awake in the other room.'

He picked up the lantern.

I followed him helplessly, calling on the gods. If he left the room with the lantern, I wouldn't last a second by myself in the darkness. My teeth would chatter with fear; I'd be sure to faint. In fact, I wouldn't be surprised if I died on the spot. My malaria-ridden spleen was already grumbling ominously.

The door to the next room stood ajar. No sooner had he entered than Kyabla cried out, 'What's this? Where are they?'

True enough—there wasn't a soul in the room. No Tenida, no Habul. Yet every door and window other than the one between the two rooms was shut tight. There was no way they could have gone out without passing through our room.

'Where can they be?' Kyabla wondered.

'The ghosts have spirited them away for certain,' I quavered. 'They must have wrung their necks and drunk their blood by now.'

Even Kyabla looked a little uncomfortable. Peering around the room, he said slowly, 'You're right, you know. Everything suddenly seems so muddled up. Can two living, breathing people vanish into thin air?'

The words were barely out of his mouth when—

A strange screeching noise came to our ears. It sounded as if a snake had caught a frog somewhere in the room. Kyabla jumped, almost dropping the lantern in his hand. I sprang into Tenida's bed.

That weird screech was heard again.

No doubt about it, these were spook sounds. My sickly spleen was in near-malarial convulsions. With my eyes shut tight, I was wondering what ghastly ghostly disaster would happen next when I heard the incongruous sound of Kyabla laughing heartily.

My eyes opened in shock. Lantern in hand, Kyabla was stooping to peer under Habul's bed. 'Here, Pela! Have a look at our leader Tenida and his friend Habul!' he grinned. 'So scared of spooks that they're hiding under the bed, holding on to each other!'

So saying, Kyabla broke into a real peal of laughter.

Their faces streaked with dust and festooned with cobwebs, Tenida and Habul crawled out from under the bed. Tenida's battleaxe of a nose seemed to be drooping a little at the tip. Habul Sen's eyes were goggling so much that they seemed in danger of falling out of his head.

'Tenida, is this what your courage has come to?' taunted Kyabla. 'You're our leader, the pride of Potoldanga, the terror of tommies on the Maidan—'

'You can stop right there.' Tenida had recovered fast. Dusting the cobwebs off his nose, he continued, 'Shut up. We hid under the bed for a reason.'

A cockroach had strayed up Habul's shoulder. Flicking it off, he agreed in forceful Dhaka accents, 'Yes, yes, a reason.'

'What reason was that? Do tell us,' challenged Kyabla in a medley of tongues. Having lived a long time in the western part of India, he often lapsed into the national language, though only for a word or two at a time.

The wind back in his sails, Tenida sat down impressively on the bed. 'Don't you see?' he began boldly. 'We were keeping watch under the bed. If a ghost or ghoul had happened to enter the room—'

'We'd have yanked its legs so hard that, ghoul or ghost—' Habul tried to take over the tale.

'—it would have been laid low,' finished Tenida.

Kyabla sniggered.

Tenida flared up. 'Laughing, are you, Kyabla? It's an insult. Take care! If you're going to be cheeky to your elders and betters, there's nothing to stop me from losing my temper and putting a spell on your—'

Tenida seemed about to try his witchcraft on Kyabla's nose when something truly terrifying happened. The

43

nearest windowpane rattled noisily. Shards of glass flew around the room and in the same instant, something that looked like a white ball shot in and bounced off the floor, coming to rest just beside Kyabla's foot.

In the light of the lantern there was no mistaking it. The object was a human skull.

'Oh brother!'

I was flat on the floor in a second. Habul and Tenida had dived back under their beds like lightning. Only Kyabla stood stock-still, with the lantern in his hand, not seeking the shelter of his bedclothes, not even sitting down.

All at once, that demonic laughter erupted again. The Jhantipahari dak bungalow trembled anew.

Who's Laughing?

What the rest of the night was like for us is best left to the imagination.

I don't know how it was with Tenida and Habul Sen—I was almost unconscious. In my swoon, it seemed as if two giant ghouls, each as tall as a coconut tree, were swinging me playfully between them. One was saying, 'We'll cook this one in a curry.' The other scoffed, 'Pooh, he's as skinny as a shrivelled shrimp. Better to treat him as a bay leaf and use him to season the dal.'

I think I was blubbering lustily when I was suddenly forced to leap up. Someone was drizzling water all over my face. Very cold water, too. Spray it on a tiger's nose, and you'd knock the poor beast senseless.

Let tigers swoon. My senses returned to me in a hurry. They had little choice in the matter.

Who could it be but Kyabla? Having fetched a watering

can from the garden, he was showering me liberally with its contents.

'Here, stop, stop!'

Would he listen? Squirting another stream of water into my face, he enquired solicitously, 'Has your brain cooled a little?'

'Not just my brain, you've cooled my entire body,' I assured him, dodging the blast of the watering can.

The morning light was glimmering through the glass windows. Our night of horror in the Jhantipahari dak bungalow had come to an end. Outside, the blue water of the lake was ruddy under a dawn sky. The sweetness of birdsong was everywhere—the dew-soaked woods of sal and palash seemed the picture of peace and beauty.

Wiping my face with the pleats of my dhoti, I wondered what harm it would have done the world if such a lovely place had remained un-haunted.

While I was meditating on these questions, Kyabla's watering can had kept up its good work. Soon enough, shrieks and yelps made me look around: worn down by the siege, Tenida and Habul were emerging from beneath the bed.

'I've found a way of recovering lost wits,' grinned Kyabla. 'Works well, doesn't it?'

'Shut up,' growled Tenida. 'Who told you we'd fainted? The two of us were laying plans in secret when you, rascal that you are, botched it all with that freezing water—'

He spluttered on a sneeze. 'You've done me in this time,' he complained. 'What with this cold morning, and your cold bath, I'll be lucky if I don't get double-pneumonia!'

Questioning Jhanturam got us nowhere.

He didn't spend nights at the bungalow. His house was a mile or more away. He had given us our dinner and gone home, only returning in the morning.

'He's no good,' said Tenida. 'As stupid as a sheep.'

'Who's to say he's not a spook himself?' mused Habul, scratching his head. 'See what he looks like. It's as if the bushy top of a coconut tree has come down to the ground.'

'Is he really a ghost then?' I exclaimed in alarm.

'And you're a pair of young ghouls,' retorted Tenida. 'Don't you know spooks vanish at the sight of fire? And this fellow lit the stove himself to make our tea, cooked that dinner of chicken curry and rice that you shovelled into your mouths with both hands. Forgotten all that, have you?'

Shovelling anything into our mouths had been out of the question last night at dinner. We had sucked on a few bones while the rest of the repast found its way into Tenida's capacious belly. But what was the use of pointing that out now?

'It doesn't matter if Jhantu is a ghost or not,' I declared. 'If we have to get ourselves killed, I'd rather perish in Potoldanga. I refuse to die at the hands of ghosts. I'm off to Kolkata this very day.'

Dhaka tones sounded an enthusiastic assent. 'Aye, aye, I was just about to say the same thing.'

Tenida began to scratch his spear-like nose.

'You and Kyabla can stay on if you want,' I said. 'The spooks can make kebabs of you, cook you into cutlets, roast you in ovens—I've no objection.'

I had made up my mind to escape that very day.

'You're right,' agreed Tenida. 'But it's such a grand place. We were eating so well, too. If only these wretched spooks hadn't spoilt everything!'

Habul waggled his head over the truth of Tenida's words. 'You're right. Don't know what pleasure they get out of haunting these jungles. If they'd make their homes in Kolkata, they could live in comfort and we'd be free of this bother. And if they'd only descend on the head pundit at school, we wouldn't have to memorize those lists of declensions!'

'Good idea, but who's going to convince them?'

Tenida sighed. 'We'll go back to Kolkata, if that's what you want. Only, it seems such a shame. Such luxury, such good food . . . have you noticed how much butter Jhantu put on our toast? A few days of this and we'd be fat.'

'Not before the spooks grew fat on us,' I pointed out.

Lifting up the plate before him, Tenida swiftly licked off a dab of butter at its very bottom. Then he heaved another heartbroken sigh.

'Today, then?'

'Today,' Habul and I spoke in unison.

We'd forgotten about Kyabla all this while. Now we realized that he had disappeared after reviving us with the miraculous Cure of the Watering Can. Where had he gone?

Tenida was alarmed. 'We haven't seen Kyabla since morning.'

'He was getting too cheeky with the ghosts. What if they've made off with him?' Habul Sen asked ominously.

Tenida screwed up his face in thought. 'They have better things to do. Not even ghosts could digest that inedible brat. But where's he got to? D'you think he's run off home without us?'

Crows dance on the roof and storks dance on the terrace
Sing the praise of Rama, surely He will spare us—

The song was so incongruous that my chair and I nearly fell over together. What new freak was this? Were the ghosts about to descend on us in broad daylight? But why on earth would ghosts sing praises of Rama?

Only it wasn't spooks. It was Kyabla. He appeared beaming from nowhere and stepped up on to the verandah.

'Where were you? And why were you bellowing like a wounded buffalo?' Tenida wanted to know.

'That's what I'm about to tell you.' Kyabla looked at our empty cups and plates in anguish. 'You've had breakfast already? Nothing left for me?'

'We don't know, Jhanturam might have something left,' said Tenida. 'You can eat breakfast later. Tell us where you've been.'

Kyabla smirked. 'In search of spooks. Didn't find any, but I did stumble on a packet of peanuts.'

'Peanuts!'

'Half a bag of nuts, and half of empty shells. That means they didn't have time to eat more.'

'Who didn't?' I asked like an idiot.

'The people sitting in the bushes outside the window, the ones who tossed in that skull. If they really were ghosts, they're fairly modern ones, Tenida. With a taste for peanuts, not to mention fritters and puffed rice. I found a greasy sal leaf and some of the puffed rice, too!'

'That means . . .' began Tenida.

'That means it's a lot of crooks trying to scare us!' Excitement made Kyabla lapse into Hindi. 'They're the ones who laughed so creepily last night and chucked that skull through the window—all to frighten us into leaving. But you're Tenida of Potoldanga, the champion who's thrashed every tommy on the Maidan . . . are you going to let these rascals frighten you away?'

'Are you sure? They really aren't ghosts?'

'Dead sure,' declared Kyabla. 'Who ever heard of ghosts munching peanuts and fritters? Smoking *beedis*, too—I found a couple of burnt-out stubs.'

'Then they're crooks all right!' Tenida of Potoldanga suddenly thumped his chest and stood up straight. 'If they're men and not spooks, I'll teach them a lesson they won't forget. Now come along, you lot—quick march—'

Tenida yanked me to my feet with such energy that I flew through the air and landed on the floor.

'Where to?' Habul still looked gloomy.

'To sort matters out with these fellows. We're Kolkata boys—do they think they can play these tricks on us and get away with it? Come on, let's have a good hunt around the place.'

'But my breakfast—' began Kyabla.

'You can have it with your lunch. Now come on!'

Habul and Kyabla had risen to their feet when, in broad daylight, at eight o'clock in the morning, something bizarre happened. A voice rasped just over our heads, 'Good, good—excellent!'

A burst of mocking laughter followed.

Who had spoken? Who had laughed? Other than the tiled roof overhead and the bare red-brick walls, there was nothing and no one to be seen. It was as if those inexplicable sounds had wafted in on a straying breeze.

Crows Dance on the Roof . . .

It wasn't night. It wasn't even dark. Cheerful sunlight shone around us. The tiled roof rose above the walls, but there wasn't even a sparrow perched on it. Yet we could have sworn that the laughter had burst terrifyingly through the tiles.

How could it be? How was this possible?

Had we lost our wits? Or had Jhantu slipped a drug into our tea? That didn't explain it—Kyabla hadn't drunk tea with us. But he'd also heard that mysterious laughter.

For nearly four minutes, your four heroes sat as dizzy as four spinning tops. Of course, it wasn't us spinning, but our wits, which whirled and sang inside our heads. We'd led a good life in Potoldanga, with its uneventful days and soothing diet of weak catfish curry. But having once fallen into Tenida's company, we were destined to die at the hands of ghosts, in remote Jhantipahari.

Another three minutes passed before my quivering spleen calmed down a little and I turned to Kyabla. 'Now what?'

Habul Sen looked up at the ceiling with eyes as round as lemons before he spoke. 'Yes, what d'you say to this?'

Tenida's scythe-shaped nose was drooping at the tip like a parrot's beak. He licked his lips nervously and mumbled, 'Yes—that is—well, if I had a man in front of me, I could punch his nose in. But with a ghost it's quite another matter, you see—'

'Besides, ghosts don't always follow boxing rules—' I struck in.

'Shut up, tiddler,' scolded Tenida.

Being called a tiddler always makes me mad. If all these ghostly goings-on hadn't left me feeling rather subdued, I'd have called Tenida a carp in return.

However, you can bend Kyabla, but you can't break him.

He was out on the front lawn in an instant. Craning his neck upwards, he seemed to be looking at something. Then, with a pleased expression, he said, 'I was right! What did I tell you? *Crows dance on the roof, and storks dance on the terrace*—'

'What d'you mean?' asked Tenida.

'I mean crows and storks dance on the roof,' repeated Kyabla.

'Stop babbling about birds and tell us what's up.'

'What do you think? It's as plain as water—someone was sitting up there on the roof and laughing in that spooky way to scare us.'

'And where did he vanish to?'

'Oh, come out here and I'll show you everything. For

heaven's sake, what are you afraid of? You can call on the gods all the while, just come!'

'Afraid? Who's afraid?' mumbled Tenida through dry lips. 'It's just these pins and needles in my foot . . .'

Kyabla chuckled.

'Yes, lots of people get pins and needles when they're scared of ghosts. I've seen quite a number of cases.'

After this, to stay in his seat would mean a serious loss of face for Tenida as a leader. With a face as pensive as a poached egg, he stepped gingerly on to the lawn. Hesitant but helpless, Habul and I followed him warily.

'See the big peepul tree at the back?' Kyabla pointed at it. 'Look how that thick branch curves right down to the roof of the bungalow. Somebody used it to climb on to the roof. He lay with his ear to the tiles, listening to our conversation, then laughed out loud to scare us and skimmed up the branch again.'

Habul nodded slowly. 'Kyabla might be right. Don't you see all those green leaves strewn over the roof? A body a-boarded that branch all right.'

'"A body a-boarded that branch all right,"' Tenida mimicked Habul's diction. 'But where did that body go?'

Kyabla said, 'They must have a den somewhere close by. I knew it as soon as I saw those peanuts and puffed rice. We'll have to hunt it out. Ready?'

Tenida scratched his nose. 'Well, the thing is—'

Kyabla sniggered again. 'The thing is that you're too scared . . . is that it? All right, if you won't come, I'll go alone.'

Preserve your dignity as leader and die a painful death!' Tenida's laugh sounded hollow. 'What rot! I tell you, if only we had a few rifles or pistols—'

A fat lot of use they'd be, I was about to point out. As if we'd ever fired rifles and pistols in our lives. Besides, put a gun into Tenida's hands and you might as well put our lives down on the expense account. He'd shoot all of us sooner than he shot a single ghost.

'Why would you need guns?' said Kyabla. 'I hear each of your famous slaps topples a tommy-soldier on the Maidan. What would a hero like you want with guns?'

At any other time, Tenida would have been delighted by this tribute. On this occasion, his pensive poached-egg expression disappeared and he looked as harassed as a hashed potato. Rather hopelessly, he said, 'All right, come on then. Let's take a look around.'

Kyabla said bracingly, 'Don't you worry, Tenida. It's bound to be the dirty work of a few rascals. Are we Potoldanga boys to be frightened off? I tell you, we'll break every bone in their bodies before we go back to Kolkata.'

Habul sighed heavily. 'Who knows whose bones will be broken?'

But Kyabla had already marched forth. His honour at stake, Tenida followed him. Habul finally scuttled after them. As for me, miserable malarial Pelaram, though I hadn't the slightest wish to enter upon this foolhardy scheme, the thought of staying behind at the bungalow by myself gave me the creeps. What if I were to hear that fiendish laughter again? It didn't bear thinking about. If only that wretched Jhanturam had been in the bungalow. But having once taken the measure of our appetites, he had served us our tea and sped off to the nearest village to buy chicken. And I wasn't the sort to sit around alone waiting for spooks to pounce on me.

But where were we going to look? And what were we expecting to find?

We set out all the same, all four of us. Thick jungle spread a long way behind the bungalow. The bushes weren't very tall—about as high as our heads, sometimes a little higher. There were stubby little sal and palash trees, and the occasional clump of wild *ghentu* or *akanda*. A fairly well-trodden trail wound through the forest. Who knew what feet had trodden it? And whether they pointed forward or backwards?

At first, my heart quaked. I kept expecting a headless spectre or a wailing banshee to emerge from the bushes. But nothing happened. A few wild fruits hung on the trees, and the loud birdsong and sweet mellow sunshine slowly wiped the fear from our minds.

I'd begun by walking fairly cautiously, sticking close to Kyabla. Then suddenly I spotted a wild berry tree. Big black fruit gleamed thick on its branches. Plucking one, I popped it into my mouth—nectar. Another followed . . . then another . . .

I had polished off about fifty when I realized the others had walked far ahead. I was hurrying to catch up with them when something made me stop. There, in the bush beside me—what was that long white thing? A bushy tail, without doubt. A squirrel's bushy tail.

Squirrels are nice little things. Bhanta's uncle had got hold of one somewhere—it went everywhere with him, perched on his shoulder or curled up in his pocket. They make terrific pets. Ever since then, I've been keen on catching one for myself. Why not grab this tail now?

Pretending to look the other way, I crept stealthily towards the bush and seized the hanging tail. Then I gave it a mighty tug.

But where was the squirrel? No sooner had I pulled on the tail than an appalling scream burst from the bushes. My ears popped. A mighty slap shot out of nowhere to land on my cheek. A spook slap!

Not just stars but planets, comets, moons and meteors all blossomed before my eyes. Then I keeled over into that very bush. As I fell, I fainted dead away. For all I could tell, I might really be dead.

That's a Beard, Not a Squirrel's Tail!

When I came to my senses, I found myself stretched out on a bed in the dak bungalow. Jhantu was fanning my head. Sitting near my feet, Kyabla blinked at me anxiously. Tenida looked solemn in a chair beside the bed.

Jhantu's fan rapped me smartly on the nose. 'Ow!' I said.

Tenida leapt out of his chair. 'Thank heavens, then you haven't passed away yet!'

'Why should he pass away?' said Kyabla. 'He'd just passed out for a bit. Didn't I say, Tenida, that we should burn a couple of chillies under Pela's nose? He'd have perked up in a minute.'

'Burn chillies indeed!' exclaimed Tenida. 'The way he was lying there with his jaw clenched, I feared he'd left Potoldanga only to perish in Jhantipahari.'

Jhantu broke in with a ghastly giggle. 'Dadababu had a fright!'

'That's enough, no need to act clever!' said Kyabla. 'Go fetch a saucerful of hot milk for Pela at once.'

Jhantu put down the fan and disappeared.

A haze still swam before my eyes. The right side of my jaw ached unbearably. That cuff had probably knocked a couple of my teeth loose. It had been a truly terrific blow. My old maths teacher's blistering slap was delicately scented Grade 3 snuff by comparison. I'm Pelaram of Potoldanga, thin as a rake, racked by malaria, forced to sustain my feeble frame on gourd-and-catfish-curry. I was finding it hard to believe that the force of that spook slap hadn't knocked my timid soul right out of my body.

Tenida addressed me. 'Now then, tiddler, what made you screech and faint away like that?'

Even in my sorry state, to be called 'tiddler' made me furious. Forgetting the ache in my jaw, I said crossly, 'I'm quite all right as a tiddler. A smack like that would have made mackerel of you!'

'Who on earth slapped you?' asked Kyabla in astonishment.

'Ghosts!'

'Ghosts!' echoed Tenida. 'As if ghosts don't have better things to do! Why would they slap you for no reason? In the middle of the morning, too! You're either batty, Pela, or bilious.'

'Bilious,' said Kyabla sagely. 'Skinny as a pole, yet he's been feasting on chicken and eggs since he got here. How could he possibly stand it? He got a touch of indigestion and it made him giddy. All this spook stuff is bogus.'

'Right,' agreed Tenida. 'I was going to say so myself.'

Nursing my jaw, I sat up in bed.

'You don't believe me, do you?'

'Not at all,' said Tenida. 'As if the spooks couldn't have found someone else to slap!'

Kyabla nodded vigorously. 'That's right. Here's our leader Tenida, with a cheek worthy of the mightiest slap, and the ghosts choose to cuff your scruffy jaw! It's an insult to the chief, understand?'

Tenida glared at Kyabla.

'Being cheeky, are you?'

Kyabla nimbly sprang about five feet away. 'Good God! Be cheeky with you?' he exclaimed, biting his tongue. 'And get my own cheek knocked in by your slap? I just meant it would be bad form for the spooks to approach anyone but the leader, whether they wanted to shake hands or have a boxing match.'

Tenida didn't seem to like the idea. Screwing up his face like semolina pudding, he snapped, 'Shut up. That's enough chat from you. But I tell you this, Pela—no more eggs for you. You're eating a stew of raw plantains and gandal leaves, and barley gruel at night. You passed out today. Tomorrow you'll pass away altogether.'

I lost my temper. 'Blast your barley gruel! I'm telling you, the spooks really slapped me! But you won't believe it.'

'Really?' Kyabla's tones were sceptical.

'That's enough, don't try to be too clever,' admonished Tenida.

'Who's being clever?' I retorted. 'Tell me why my right cheek's still aching then.'

'It just is,' answered Tenida. 'Don't people feel their teeth chatter and their heads spin and their ears buzz for no reason? Have they all been attacked by ghosts?'

I felt extremely hurt. I'd gone to the trouble of getting myself slapped by a spook, but these wretches just wouldn't believe me. Well, none of them had a slap to boast of. They were probably just jealous.

'Why won't you believe me?' I demanded hotly. 'You lot had gone on ahead. I'd just eaten a few berries when I noticed a squirrel's tail waving in the bushes. I grabbed hold of it and all of a sudden—'

'—the squirrel slapped you, did it?' Tenida roared with laughter. Kyabla snickered through his nose with a noise like jackals squabbling in a bush.

At this insult, my sickly spleen danced in my stomach with rage. But just then, I happened to glance at my right hand. It was clutching a mass of long white hairs! A bit of the tail must have come away in my grip.

I stretched my hand out. 'Here! Look what's still sticking to my palm!'

Kyabla was in front of me with a single bound. Tenida's paw swiped the hair from mine.

Then Tenida cried out, 'But this . . . this is—'

'—a beard!' cried Kyabla, even louder.

'A white beard,' added Tenida.

'Stained with red,' Kyabla pointed out. 'A tobacco-stained beard.'

'A ghost's beard,' said Tenida.

'A tobacco-smoking ghost's beard,' said Kyabla.

A ghost's beard! The words made my limbs curl into my stomach with fear. What a disaster! What had I done? Thinking I was grabbing a squirrel's tail, had I yanked out a spook's beard instead? No doubt that was what earned me that terrific slap. But would the slap be all? Who knew how tenderly that beard had been cherished? Perhaps its owner had mooned away whole nights in a *shaora* tree, stroking it and humming melodies in Raag Khamaj. Of course, I wasn't very sure what Raag Khamaj sounded like, but the name was enough to convince me that only spook songs could do justice to it. Now that I'd ruined that precious beard, I'd be lucky if the ghosts didn't pluck my hair out by the roots tonight. Let Kyabla and Tenida meditate on its mysteries. My arms and legs went limp and I fell back on the bed.

Examining the hair with great attention, Kyabla asked suddenly, 'But Tenida, do ghosts smoke tobacco?'

'What's to stop them?'

'Well, you see, the thing is . . .' Kyabla scratched his head and lapsed into Hindi, 'it's just that I've heard ghosts can't stand fire . . . how do they light their pipes then? And besides, there's something very familiar about this beard—reddish-white, tobacco-stained. I've seen it somewhere before . . .'

Kyabla was going to say more when suddenly, holding a pair of shoes in his hand, Jhantu stepped into the room. Thrusting them under Tenida's nose, he began, 'Look, Dadababu—'

'Where did they find a loon like you?' Tenida let out a roar. 'We told you to fetch some hot milk for Pela and you bring me a pair of shoes! D'you expect me to sit here chewing on them?'

'God forbid!' exclaimed Jhantu piously. 'It's dogs that should chew on shoes, not you! I was just wondering where Habul Babu had gone. His shoes were lying outside, but he was nowhere to be seen. Then I noticed a letter in one shoe, so I brought you the pair.'

A letter in a shoe? And true enough! I hadn't seen Habul in the room since I'd come around.

'He's right,' said Kyabla. 'There does seem to be a note in that shoe. What d'you think is up, Tenida? And where's Habul disappeared to?'

Tenida pulled out the piece of folded-up paper. 'Pipe down, peanut,' he admonished. 'Let me see what this says.'

But no sooner had he glanced over the note than Tenida's eyes seemed to start from his head. He gulped three times in succession before managing to say, 'Brother Kyabla, we're done for.'

'Done for? What d'you mean?'

'I mean Habul's gone.'

'Gone where?' Kyabla and I cried out together. 'What's in that note, Tenida? What does it say?'

'Listen,' said Tenida hoarsely. 'I'll read it aloud.'
The note said:

We have made Habul Sen Vanish Mysteriously. On receiving this note, if you pack up your possessions and return immediately to Kolkata, Habul will be restored to you unharmed. If not, we will make all four heroes of Potoldanga Vanish permanently. We warn you of this in advance. Do not blame us later.

Yours, etc

Chop Yu Thin Lee, Barbaric Chinese Bandit

The Band of 'Hu Yu Fu Ling?'

Tenida sat down heavily on the floor. A large bumblebee had been hovering about his nose for a while now, probably thinking that its magnificent dimensions would support a hive of some size. But the nose now emitted a startling rumble, frightening the poor creature so much that it shot three feet away.

Our leader was clearly in a sorry state. In a small voice, he said, 'Oh help! We've had it! To fall into the hands of Chinese bandits in the end! Better spooks than this!'

I felt as if my limbs had tied themselves into a knot at the centre of my sickly spleen.

'A bandit called Chop Yu Thin Lee, too!' I quavered. 'That means he'll cut us into little pieces.'

Jhantu had been standing there blinking at us. Astonished by our woeful state, he asked 'What's the matter, Dadababu?'

'The matter? The matter's beyond belief! Look here, Jhantu, are there dacoits in these parts?'

'Dacoits?' exclaimed Jhantu. 'What would dacoits do here? We've neither dacoits nor robbers hereabouts!'

'No indeed!' snapped Tenida, looking as cross as a curried yam. 'Then where did Chop Yu Thin Lee come from? Not any old sinner either, but a Barbaric Chinese Bandit!'

What a spunky young brat our Kyabla was! Nothing seemed to shake him. Now he said, 'Oh rubbish, forget all this nonsense! Don't you see, it's all a hoax. Sheer bluster! As if Chop Yu Thin Lee wouldn't have better things to do than fool around a bungalow in the hills of Hazaribagh! Do you know what this is really like? A Bengali detective novel!'

'A Bengali detective novel?' mused Tenida, scratching his chin. 'What d'you mean?'

'What do you think I mean? All those detective thrillers with submarines surfacing in ponds and world-conquering supermen for sleuths . . . that's where all this comes from. My uncle's an officer at Lalbazar—I once asked him where such detectives were to be found. He flew into a rage and snapped, "In a hubble-bubble."'

'To hell with your detectives!' exclaimed Tenida irritably. 'What have they got to do with Chop Yu Thin Lee?'

'Everything,' answered Kyabla with an air of omniscience. 'Whoever wrote that note definitely reads detective stories. He's picked up all his tricks from them.'

'But what's the point? Why do they want to drive us away? And where have they taken Habul?'

'That's the mystery,' replied Kyabla. 'The one we have to solve. There must be some bad men about, and close by, too. But they've done us a real favour by leaving us this note, Tenida.'

'A favour?' exclaimed Tenida. 'What favour?'

'Well, it's made one thing clear. There isn't a ghost or ghoul for miles—that's all poppycock. A few crooks are lurking around and they need this house for their dirty work.' Kyabla puffed out his chest. 'But can a couple of rogues scare away Potoldanga boys? We'll beat them at their own game and show the band of "Chop Yu Thin Lee" that we're the band of "Hu Yu Fu Ling?"!'

'Hu Yu Fu Ling?' I echoed. 'Who're they?'

'Diabolic Chinese Bandits,' answered Kyabla. 'One notch above the Barbaric kind.'

'When did we turn Chinese?' I asked rather aggrievedly. 'And why on earth should we be bandits?'

'If they can be Chinese, why not us?' countered Kyabla. 'We'll be Chinese of the choicest sort. If they're banditti, we'll be bandittoes.'

'Bandittoes?' The bee was making a beeline for Tenida's nose again. Trying to swat it away, Tenida asked, 'What's a banditto?'

'Exactly like a bandit—ditto but deadlier. Ordinary bandits are snuff to them.'

Tenida stood up. 'Look here, Kyabla, don't try to be funny about everything. If these are really bandits—'

'If they were really bandits, they'd have proved their mettle by this time. They wouldn't be sitting in bushes munching peanuts and chucking paper-wrapped skulls about. They're cowards of the first order.'

'Then how did they manage to make off with Habul Sen?'

'By some sneaky trick, no doubt. But it won't take us long to learn their ways. Tenida—'

'What?'

'We can't wait any longer. Are you ready?'

'Ready for what?'

'To see how Chop Yu Thin Lee answers the challenge of Hu Yu Fu Ling, this very minute.'

Tenida didn't seem particularly eager. He shrank visibly and asked, 'How will we do that?'

'We'll manage it. They must have a den fairly close to this bungalow. We'll have to attack it.'

'What if they fire pistols and things?'

'We'll throw brickbats,' Kyabla stuck his tongue out. 'Pistols indeed! Popping out every minute in detective novels. D'you think they come so cheap? But a couple of cudgels would be handy. Here Jhantu, got any stout sticks?'

Jhantu had been listening to us in silence. Goodness knows what he'd made of our exchange, but now he nodded his head and answered, 'Two. And a club as well.'

'Then fetch them here quick.'

'What d'you want with clubs and cudgels, Dadababu?' he asked in bewilderment.

'We're going to hunt foxes.'

'Foxes?' exclaimed Jhantu. 'But why? D'you fancy the meat?'

'Is it any of your business?' retorted Kyabla, annoyed. 'Do as I tell you! Bring us those sticks and be quick about it.'

Jhantu went off to fetch the cudgels and clubs. In a rather hollow voice, Tenida began, 'Kyabla, perhaps this isn't a good idea. If we really do run into danger . . .'

Kyabla screwed up his nose in disdain. 'Scared, are you? All right, you sit here in the bungalow. I'm setting out, and Pela, sickly wretch as he is, will come with me. You'll find even he's got more pluck than you.'

My chest swelled with pride at Kyabla's words, but my spleen wobbled a little. Would I have to go, too? Well, go I would! After all, you only died once.

And if I did die . . . all right, Mother would cry, so would Aunt, and the Board of Secondary Examinations would probably shed a few tears as well, for who'd pay the fees to sit the school final every year? And daily sales at the local market would be reduced by half a measure of potol and four catfish. A bunch of *basak* leaves might be saved, too. So be it. The world could well sustain such trifling losses for the sake of my heroic self-sacrifice.

Tenida sighed heavily. 'All right, let's go. But that beard of Pela's—'

'Tobacco-stained beard,' I corrected.

Kyabla said, 'Right. In fact, that beard is further proof that these rogues aren't remotely Chinese. Why, there are so many Chinese folk in Kolkata . . . ever seen one with a beard?'

True enough! A Chinaman with a beard? None of us had ever seen such a thing.

In the meantime, Jhantu had assembled his arsenal. He shouldered the club himself, Kyabla seized one stick and Tenida the other. What was I left with? A piece of firewood lay at hand, so I picked it up. If I had to die, I wouldn't go without striking a blow or two.

Thus the warrior band of Hu Yu Fu Ling sallied out, the light of battle in its eye, to avenge itself on the band of Chop Yu Thin Lee. Once more we took the forest trail, beating every bush we passed to see if it concealed some tobacco-smoking enemy.

But it wasn't long before I got myself into new trouble. It wasn't wild berries this time. It was star plums.

We had started out just beyond the bungalow. I was lagging behind the others as usual. Of course, it had to be my eye that fell on the bush of star plums. Ah, it was positively glowing with fruit!

A seer of water flooded my mouth. Endless spells of fever had left me craving sour things from the depths of my soul. Forgetting Chop Yu Thin Lee, I scuttled up to the tree. One never gets to eat star plums in Kolkata. Faced with this magnificent array, who wouldn't lose his head? But as soon as I set foot under the tree . . .

Ugh! My foot landed in a large pat of cow dung, and I went flying. But what was this? Instead of landing with a bump on the ground, I seemed to be hurtling through space, plunging into the depths of hell. Only it wasn't hell either. I found myself beached high on a massive shoulder. And letting out a yelp of 'Oh brother!' its owner went sprawling with me to the ground.

I passed out once more.

Gajeswar's Prisoners

Being unconscious isn't a bad thing unless a tree-ant happens to bite you. And if an entire swarm of ants begins digging into you at once, what then? Forget fainting fits, even a dead man would leap up in a trice.

I sprang up too.

A smoky darkness surrounded me. I could hardly make out anything at first. A mist floated before my eyes. Another tree-ant bit me quite unnecessarily on the left ear.

'*Baap re*!' I shrieked, and flicked the ant off.

At once someone laughed with a curious clicking noise, like a bullfrog croaking. Then, in a horse-like whinny, he said, 'Calling on your father at the bite of a tree-ant! At this rate, if a wasp were to sting you, you'd have to call upon your uncle-by-marriage!'

Standing only a couple of yards away, a man built like a wrestler watched me, alert as a hunting badger's waiting paw. Now he laughed like a croaking frog again.

Everything seemed very strange to me. 'Where am I?' I asked.

'"Where am I?"' mimicked the man, mockingly baring a brace of horribly large teeth. Then in rasping tones, like a pair of squabbling owls, he snapped, 'Innocent, aren't you? You look as if butter wouldn't melt in your mouth! Landing on my back like a falling coconut, then asking sweetly, "Where am I?" Can't you play the fool somewhere else?'

Everything suddenly came back to me. The star plums, my stealthy approach, my fatal slip in the cow dung . . . and then . . .

'Have I fallen into the hands of Chop Yu Thin Lee?' I wailed.

'Chop Yu . . .? What on earth is that?' the words slipped out before the man could collect himself. 'Yes, yes, so you have! Babaji did write a letter saying something like that.'

'Babaji? What Babaji?'

'You'll know soon enough,' the man bared his teeth at me again. 'Think you're smart, don't you? We've worn ourselves out telling you to go away—tried to scare you away with spooks, sat in that bush an entire night, throwing skulls at you and being bitten to death by mosquitoes, grown hoarse laughing those creepy laughs, but did you take heed? Just you wait! I've nabbed one of you already. Now you've also walked into the trap. I'll make *sheekh kabab* of you, I will.'

'What? Sheekh kabab!'

'Or alu kabli, if I feel like it. Or chicken cutlets. You might make a good chop, too.' The man scratched his head

73

worriedly. 'I only wonder—are you fit to eat? I've seen lots of urchins in my day, but never such an inedible-looking bunch as you.'

Hearing this gave me a little hope. I was fated to die, but a last try wouldn't hurt.

'You're quite right,' I began. 'Don't eat any of us—me in particular. You'll never digest me if you do. In fact, you'll probably get cholera or break out in rashes or die of diphtheria. Shivering fits and hot flushes wouldn't surprise me either.'

'Pipe down, you puppy,' retorted the man. 'Don't talk too much. For the moment, I'm putting you in cold storage with your friend Habul Sen. You can stay there for a while. Later, once Babaji has returned, and I've snared the rest of your friends, we'll decide whether to make *Mughlai parathas* of you or beat you like eggs into a pudding.'

'I beg of you, Baba,' I pleaded, 'don't eat me. You won't enjoy it. I've got chronic malaria. All I eat is weak catfish curry with gourd. There isn't a drop of juice in my flesh. My maths teacher Gopi Babu says even Yama's allergic to me. You'll eat me only to die before your time, Baba Chop-Yu-Thin-Lee—'

My captor lost his temper. 'Oh blast your Chop Yu Thin Lee! Why, my fine fellow, what made you polish off my guru's rasagollas in the train to Ranchi? When you cleaned out his pot of holy snakes, I suppose you didn't think you'd have us to reckon with one day! If I hadn't slipped on that banana skin at Muri station . . .'

By now, I was gaping at him. My eyes weren't just wide, they were goggling with shock.

'Heavens, then you're . . .'

'Recognized me at last? I'm Guru Gloomyswami's unworthy disciple, Gajeswar Garui.'

'Oh brother!'

Gajeswar smiled a little. 'You thought you'd got away as soon as the train pulled out of Muri, didn't you? You didn't know we'd followed by the next train. Now you'll see what's what.'

Fear turned my blood to water. I could tell that all was up for Pelaram of Potoldanga. This villain Gajeswar would make shammi kabab of me for sure. But then, if I was going to die, it was no use being frightened. Better to strike up a conversation with Gajeswar.

'But what are you doing here? What do you want with Uncle's bungalow? Why're you lurking in this little hollow on the hillside? Well, all right, lurk if you want to. But what made you dump a mound of the most revolting cow dung at the edge of the hole?'

'As if we put it there!' retorted Gajeswar crossly. 'A cow did! For idiots like you to slip on, probably.'

'Very likely—but why do you want to drive us away? What do you want with the house?'

'Why d'you want to know, eh, little shrimp? Pinch your nose and it'll drip milk. What will you get out of knowing our plans?' Gajeswar yawned disgustedly.

A shrimp? How dare he! Another tree-ant drove its sting

into my right ear like an injection needle. With an '*ow*' I yanked it off and sternly addressed Gajeswar.

'Look, make chops and cutlets of me if you like, but don't you call me a shrimp.'

'Why not? I'll call you a shrimp cutlet,' Gajeswar smiled slyly.

'No you won't,' I retorted. 'And my nose doesn't drip milk. I've sat the school finals twice already.'

'Heavens, he's sat the school finals!' Gajeswar produced a beedi from a waist pouch and lit it. 'All right, tell me—what does "cataclysm" mean?'

'Cataclysm? *Cata*clysm.' I scratched my nose. 'Kittens, I suppose.'

'My foot!' snorted Gajeswar, puffing out a cloud of smoke. 'All right, name the capital of Senegambia.'

'It must be Honolulu,' I answered promptly. 'Or perhaps it's Madagascar?'

'Guzzled your geography like *golguppas*, haven't you?' Gajeswar screwed up his nose. 'What's the meaning of *jadyapaha*, eh? Whom would you call *aniket*?'

'What's that—Animesh? Why, he's my cousin!'

'That's enough!' Gajeswar snapped at me like an angry owl again. 'Why just the school finals? You'll fail the scholarship exam, too! No, I find you really aren't fit to eat. Perhaps one could throw a few odds and ends of you into a bitter *shukto*. Now get up.'

'Where do I have to go?'

'Into cold storage, as I told you. Your friend Habul Sen is

there already: you'll meet him again. Meanwhile, Gurudev and the other men have gone out to take care of some business. Once he returns, we'll see . . .'

I'd been looking around me all this while. In this moment of crisis, Pelaram of Potoldanga's wits had cleared a little. I needed to know where exactly I had landed.

As far as I could tell, I had fallen into a hollow in the hillside, about seven or eight feet deep. If I hadn't landed on Gajeswar's back, my bones would have been ground to powder. At the moment, I was sitting at the mouth of a tunnel of some kind. Where it went, or how far, I couldn't tell. But somewhere down there was the cold store, and in it, Habul Sen.

Habul's rescue would have to wait. But couldn't I escape? Was there no way of getting out?

The round hole through which I'd tumbled gaped above my head like the mouth of a well. Looking at it carefully, I noticed handy notches cut into the surrounding stones. With a little effort one could jump up and . . .

A couple of minutes went by as I pondered routes of escape. Gajeswar finished his beedi and began looking at me with a beady eye.

'I say, what's the idea? Think you'll get away? You can put paid to that plan! You might escape from a tiger, but you won't give Gajeswar Garui the slip. On top of that, you've yanked out my guru's beard. There's no telling what your fate might be—' Gajeswar pulled a ghastly face at me and got to his feet.

Heavens! That tobacco-stained ghostly beard was the Great Gloomyswami's! Then it was the swami who'd been lurking in the bush, and his sacred beard that I'd mistaken for a squirrel's tail.

'I didn't pull it on purpose!' I whimpered. 'I thought—'

'That's enough, I don't need to know what you thought. The pain in his cheek made Gurudev restless for two whole hours. When he gets back . . . no, let that be. Come on now—'

Unfurling an arm like an elephant's trunk, Gajeswar was about to grab me, when suddenly he screamed, 'Baap re, I'm done for!'

By then I'd noticed it too. Black as ink, pincers still upraised, a big scorpion stood like a little god of death by Gajeswar's foot.

'I'm done for, I'm burning up—'

So saying, that ox of a man began to roll on the ground like a pumpkin. 'I'm finished, I'm finished—it's killed me—'

And I? Would I get such a chance again? One quick bound, and I had set my foot in the steps carved into the hillside. It was now or never!

Seth Dhunduram

Jack be nimble, Jack be quick!

By the time I'd reached the mouth of the hole, stepping from cleft to cleft, my sickly spleen was hopping like a turtle in my stomach. Not that I'd ever seen turtles hop—all they did was wriggle and poke their heads out of their shells. But if a turtle ever did happen to hop—to lift up its limbs and dance around in joy—it would have danced exactly as my spleen was dancing now. In fact, it danced for five whole minutes.

When it stopped, I held on to a branch of the star plum tree and looked around. Not a soul in sight. There was no telling where Tenida and Kyabla were. Perched in the *amra* tree opposite, a monkey pulled a face at me. I returned the compliment by baring my teeth and grimacing horribly. The monkey grew very cross and said 'Chitter, chitter—squeak!' It probably meant to say, 'You've got some cheek!' Then it scuttled into the leaves and vanished.

Gajeswar's Garui's groans were floating up through the hole at my feet. I quite liked the sound. The blighter had sworn to make cutlets of me. Quizzed me on the meanings of horrible English words and asked me what the capital of Senegambia was. It served him right. A hill scorpion's sting would make Gajeswar sing for three whole days now!

My eye fell again on that fatal pat of cow dung. My foot had made a clear streak through it when I slipped. Yes, it was that cursed mess that had sent me flying hell-wards. Feeling very angry, I stamped hard on it to teach it a lesson.

Ugh, what had I done? Fine fresh cow dung it was! It splattered right into my face. Damn and blast!

But it didn't seem advisable to hang around here. There was no telling with Gajeswar—what if he suddenly emerged from that hole? The best idea was to make tracks at once.

But which way should I go? I knew I was somewhere just behind the Jhantipahari bungalow, but how was I to reach it? The toss I'd taken seemed to have scrambled all memories of our outward route into semolina pudding inside my head. Should I go left or right? Moreover, I have one terrible fault. As soon as I step outside the precincts of Potoldanga, I can't tell east from west or north from south. Once, on a trip to Deoghar, I said to my cousin, 'Look, Phuchu da, what an astonishing thing! What a splendid sunrise that is in the north!' Phuchu da immediately clipped my long ear. 'Off you go to Ranchi, Pela! You're bound for the lunatic asylum.'

I was wondering which way to go when my eyes grew as round as syrup balls with shock. Who were those people creeping towards me from the other side of the forest? Whose beard was that fluttering like a squirrel's tail in the breeze?

Without doubt, it was the Great Gloomyswami! Followed by two other ox-like men, with two mysterious-looking covered clay pots in their hands. Pots of holy snakes, I was sure. The kind likely to contain curd and rasagollas. They couldn't be planning to eat it all themselves—no doubt Habul Sen would come in for a share.

I'm Pelaram of Potoldanga. Rasagollas have always been my weakness. But greed wasn't going to make me walk into Gajeswar Garui's hands again—no, never! Better to scoot if it saved my skin.

I slipped swiftly into the bush beside me. Running was impossible . . . they'd hear my footsteps. I began to shuffle stealthily through the bush.

On and on I went. I had no idea which way I was going. Past shrubs and bushes, hopping over ditches, almost falling over a little fox, I scuttled along. Fall into the clutches of bandit chief Chop Yu Thin Lee again, and I was finished! Given the temper Gajeswar was in, he'd make mincemeat of me in a trice.

After walking blindly for almost an hour, I reached a little stream. Its blue water rippled through fine loose sand strewn with rocks and pebbles. My legs felt as if they were about to fall off—my throat was as parched as dry wood.

I sat down on a rock and rested awhile. The sky had clouded over, and this was a nice shady spot. I began to feel blissfully comfortable. Woods of palash were all around me. Across the little river, I could see a pair of blue jays.

I even drank a little water from the stream. Deliciously cool, and just as sweet, it perked me up immediately. Barbaric Bandit Chop Yu Thin Lee, Gajeswar, Tenida, Kyabla, Habul—I forgot them all. I felt so fine that I wanted to sing. Ta ra ra ra—rama ho, rama ho—

I had just struck up a fine melody in ta-ra-ra-ra-s when suddenly, from behind me, there was a *parp-parp-parp*!

Blast the noise—it had completely ruined my mood for music! And, more importantly, where had a motor car sprung from in the godforsaken jungles of Jhantipahari?

Looking carefully, I found there was a track running along the riverbank. And indeed, a blue motor car stood in the shade of the palash trees a little further down it.

Good grief—were they also Chop Yu Thin Lee's men? After all, you did read of things like this in detective stories! A remote forest—a mysterious motor car—three men in black masks with pistols in their hands—and Detective Himadri Roy staring at it all. My malarial spleen did a belly flip at the mere thought. In fact, it seemed on the point of beginning its turtle jig again.

I was thinking of jumping up and running for my life when the *parp, parp, parp* sounded again. The motor car blew its horn. And the figure that climbed down from it left me gaping. No, such a man couldn't possibly be a bandit. In no detective novel would you ever find such a character!

He had an enormous, wobbling paunch—a crane would

snap if it tried to lift him. An entire bolt of cloth must have gone into the making of the silk kurta on his massive form. His eyes and nose were sunk deep into a great balloon of a face. On his head he wore a massive yellow turban. No scope for a neck—his head seemed to emerge directly from his belly. A gold chain glittered just below his chin. Ten rings sparkled on ten fat fingers.

A Sethji, large as life and twice as natural.

No, he couldn't possibly be one of Bandit Chop Yu Thin Lee's men. In fact, he seemed exactly the sort to attract a bandit's attention. But what had possessed this perfect specimen of a Sethji to wander into these jungles?

The Sethji called out in nasal tones, '*Khonka*! O *khonka*!'

He seemed to be calling me. There certainly wasn't another young lad in sight. I thought it over quickly and scuttled cautiously towards him.

'Namaste, Sethji.'

'Namaste, khonka.' The Sethji seemed to smile. Several teeth and two twinkling eyes winked briefly in the balloon-like face. He inquired, 'Who are you belonging to? And doing what in this forest?'

At first, I thought of telling him the truth. Then I reflected that you never knew a man's real intentions. This Jhantipahari didn't seem a comfortable sort of place. For all I knew, the Sethji's massive belly might conceal a perfect horror house of mysteries.

So I promptly answered, 'We are studying in a school in Hazaribagh. And coming here for a picnic.'

'*Haan*! Coming here to picnic?' The Sethji's eyes twinkled in the balloon again. 'Coming so far? And where are all the other boys being?'

'They're being somewhere there,' I pointed in a random direction. Then I asked in turn, 'And who are you being? Why being in this jungle?'

'Myself?' pronounced the Sethji. 'Myself being Seth Dhunduram. My shop is being in Kolkata—also being in Ranchi. I am coming here to collect taxes on this forest.'

'Oh, to collect taxes on the forest?' I felt a sudden urge to pull the Sethji's leg. 'But don't wander too far, Sethji— I've heard that bears have been getting up to all kinds of mischief in these parts.'

'Bears!' Seth Dhunduram's paunch gave a little jump. 'Bears are biting people?'

'Biting like fury,' I assured him. 'Biting all the time.'

'What!'

'Biting harder when seeing big belly,' I told the Sethji comfortingly. 'Bears are liking to bite bellies. But don't you be worrying.'

'What! Ram, Ram!'

The Sethji jumped in shock. If I hadn't seen him do it, I wouldn't have believed a figure like his capable of a bound like that.

Then that silk-covered two-tonne sack sprinted to the car and scrambled in. No sooner was he aboard than he yelled, 'O Chhaganlal, be starting up the motor! Quick!'

Parp-parp! In the wink of an eye, Seth Dhunduram's blue motor car had disappeared into the jungle. For a full five minutes, I stood and chuckled happily. A fine prank I'd played!

But the grin was soon wiped off my face. Suddenly, from the bushes just behind me, there came a—

Halooom!

Not a bear, but a bear's big brother. A tiger! Who was to know that jokes could turn so horribly real?

'Baap re, I've had it!' So saying, I made a wild spring myself. Wilder than even the Sethji's leap.

With a loud splash, I plunged into the icy water of the stream. And once more, right behind me, there rose a deafening roar: 'Halooom!'

Tiger Trouble

Good God, what freezing water! My very bones shook with the cold. There was a strong current too. I had gone in up to my knees, but in no time at all, it had pulled me about thirty yards downstream.

But it was either cold water or hungry tiger: I'd be a tasty snack for the latter if I stopped. Floundering across the stream, I caught my foot on a stone and fell flat on my face in the water, swallowing a fair amount. I was certain the tiger would pounce on me any minute, when I heard a roar—of laughter, not a tiger—behind me.

A laughing tiger? Could tigers laugh? I'd seen lots of tigers in the zoo. They gobbled greedily or growled grumpily or slept soundly. Many a time had I stood by the bars wondering if tigers ever snored and what it sounded like if they did. I'd even hatched a plan to throw a saucerful of snuff at a tiger's nose, in an earnest desire to hear it sneeze. Only, my cousin Phuchu da had snatched the saucer from me and rapped me smartly on the head. But never in my wildest dreams had I thought I'd hear a tiger laugh.

I was thinking of turning around to take a look at this peculiar beast when I skidded on some pebbles and landed in the water again. The laughter broke out once more. A voice called, 'Now get up, Pela, that's enough. You'll die of double-pneumonia this time.'

It was no tiger's voice.

Who else? It had to be Kyabla, with Tenida beside him. They stood side by side, wearing grins as toothy as rows of tubers.

Screwing up his long nose, Tenida jeered, 'To leap into the river just because I let out a tiger's roar or two! You're such a coward, Pela!'

So they'd been playing tigers to fool me, had they? Villains! They'd got me soaked for no reason at all. Now I was shivering all over.

Mad as fire, I climbed out of the river. 'What d'you think you're doing?' I demanded.

'What do *you* think you're doing?' countered Kyabla. 'One minute you're crawling after us, happy as a snail, and the next you're gone! We went frantic looking for you. In the end we found you sitting here, laughing like a lunatic. So we decided to have a little laugh ourselves at your expense.'

'Did you think I'd vanished on purpose?' I retorted. 'I fell into the bandit Chop Yu Thin Lee's pit!'

'Bandit Chop Yu Thin Lee's pit! What on earth is that?' The two of them stared at me open-mouthed.

'Or you could call it the Great Gloomyswami's snare.'

'The Great Gloomyswami?' Kyabla gulped three times in succession. Tenida stared at me with his mouth open, like a cawing crow.

'And Gajeswar Garui's in it as well. That man like an elephant.'

'What?'

'Seth Dhunduram's blue motor car too.'

'*What?*'

Seeing them gaping like idiots, I felt very pleased. I even considered striking up another ta-ra-ra-ra. But an icy blast seemed to be whistling around my innards. My merry tune would emerge as a startling vibrato. 'Let's go back to the bungalow,' I said. 'I'll tell you everything there.'

They could hardly believe my story when they heard it. The Great Gloomyswami and Bandit Chop Yu Thin Lee the same person? Gajeswar Garui in the gang as well? The whole lot encamped in a cave on the mountainside? Tell us another!

'No doubt Pela's malaria came back while he was wandering around the jungle,' declared Tenida. 'He dreamt all this up while he was delirious.'

'All right, so it was a dream,' I retorted. 'Let the scorpion's sting stop burning and Gajeswar Garui will be here again. You're our leader. He'll make fowl cutlets of you first.'

'Fowl means chicken,' mused Kyabla. 'You can't call Tenida a chicken—he doesn't have wings. You might call him a goat, though. The problem is that goats have four legs. Tenida, could your arms be called a pair of legs?'

Tenida dealt out a slap. Only it landed on the back of Kyabla's chair instead of on his head. Tenida danced about in agony for a few seconds.

When he had stopped dancing, he said, 'It was a mistake to bring you loons with me in the first place. On top of that, there's no telling where that pest Habul's got to. How can I look after everything on my own?'

'Look after things!' Kyabla exclaimed. 'We've found out what kind of leader you are. The real question is, who'll look after you?'

Tenida raised his hand for another slap, and Kyabla promptly shot out of his chair.

'Yes, go on squabbling!' I said angrily. 'While Gajeswar makes chops out of Habul.'

'Mutton chops,' said Kyabla. 'Habul's a goat if there ever was one. But it's time we got going, Tenida. Let's find out if Pela's telling the truth. Come on, Pela. Let's see where it is, the Gloomyswami's hidey-hole. Up you get, Tenida, quick!'

Tenida scratched his nose, 'Wait a minute, let me think.'

'What's there to think about?' asked Kyabla. 'Ready? Quick march! One, two, three—'

Tenida looked as if someone had given him a stiff dose of quinine. 'I mean ... I was thinking ... should we venture into that cave just as we are? We haven't got more than a bunch of sticks amongst us. Those men could be armed with pistols! And they might have a lot of thugs in their gang. There's just the three of us. Even Jhantu's gone off to the market ...'

Kyabla puffed out his chest and stood very straight.

'What's the worst that can happen, Tenida? They can't do more than kill us, can they? Better die a hero than live a coward. Leave our friend in danger and run away for fear of a lot of goons? We're Potoldanga boys!'

You won't believe it. But looking at Kyabla's blazing eyes, I suddenly felt much braver. He was right—do or die! Why live the life of a malaria-stricken mouse? For shame! After all, I wouldn't die twice.

Glancing at Tenida, I saw he was standing proudly erect. Gone was that trembling form—he was the terror of tommy-soldiers again, the champion of the Maidan. His voice was a tiger's roar. 'You're right, Kyabla; you've brought my wisdom teeth out today. Not one, but a pair of them. I'll get Habul Sen safely back to Kolkata or perish!'

That's what you call a leader! The very man we needed!

We set out at once. Tenida and Habul were already gripping a pair of stout sticks, but I had lost my broken branch. All I could do was grab a length of wood and follow them.

This time there was no mistaking the place. There was the tree of star plums, there the evil pat of cow dung that had sent me flying. But the cave? Where had the cave gone?

There was no sign of an opening in the hillside. Just a mass of bushes.

'Well, where's your cave?' demanded Kyabla.

Where indeed?

Tenida broke in. 'I told you at the start—Pela, you dreamt it all up in a delirious fit! The Great Gloomyswami a Chinese Bandit? Your brain's as fried as an onion fritter.'

My head was spinning madly. Had it really all been a feverish dream? Then why was I still aching all over? My slipping foot had left a clear streak in the cow dung. What about that?

Was it the work of ghosts? Birds can fly away, rasagollas melt in the mouth, chops and cutlets vanish like twinkling into hungry stomachs. But I'd never heard of an entire cave melting into thin air.

Tenida said jestingly, 'You see, Pela? Your cave vanished in fear at the sight of us!' He kicked boldly at a bush. At once, an earthquake seemed to erupt under it.

But Tenida seemed seized by an even fiercer convulsion. With a startled cry, he disappeared with the bush into the bowels of the mountain. It was like the earth engulfing Sita. We could hear muffled noises below—scrabble, scratch, thump!

Then those weren't bushes after all but branches cut from trees to cover the mouth of the cave!

Kyabla and I stood there dumbfounded, not knowing what to say or do.

Tenida's yells floated up from the depths of the tunnel: 'Kyabla, Pela!'

We yelled back, 'What news, Tenida?'

'I've got a few bumps, nothing much. Quick, step in the cracks and climb down the rocks! There's something terrible here, a hair-raising sight!'

Our own hair stood on end at the words. I remembered my resolution—do or die! Stepping into the mouth of the cave, I began climbing down, Kyabla just behind me.

The Corpse of Habul Sen

Kyabla and I soon reached the cave. But we couldn't see a soul once we were in it. Not Tenida, not Gajeswar—not a hair of the Great Gloomyswami's torn-out beard.

What could have happened? Had the dastardly band of Chop Yu Thin Lee made Tenida vanish as well?

Kyabla looked blankly at me. 'Tenida just fell down this hole! Where's he gone?'

I was looking carefully around the dim cave for that hill scorpion, though. For all I knew it was lurking in some corner with its tail raised to sting. That monster of a Gajeswar had barely survived one swift strike. Miserable malarial Pelaram of Potoldanga would give up the ghost in a trice.

Kyabla thumped me on the head. 'I say, where's Tenida gone?'

'How would I know?'

'Very fishy!' mused Kyabla, scratching his nose. 'Has he melted into thin air?'

Tenida of Potoldanga? Our mighty leader? Was he the sort that just disappeared into the air? Though he remained invisible, his voice rang out at once. 'Kyabla, Pela, come here quick! It's a disaster, I tell you!'

Go where? Where could he be calling from? This was really getting spooky. My hair pricked up in terror.

Kyabla yelled, 'Tenida, where are you? We can't see you at all!'

Tenida's tones floated back. 'Downstairs!'

'Downstairs?'

'Are you blind?' growled Tenida. 'Can't you see the gap in the wall in front of you?'

Why, there it was! A gap in the stone wall facing us! Going closer, we saw a ladder set into the stone. This place was turning out to be quite a palace of mystery.

'Climb down,' called Tenida. 'It's a terrible business, I tell you. Makes your hair stand on end.'

Help!

Kyabla went down the ladder first. I followed. Tenida was right, there really was a 'downstairs'. We found ourselves in something like a long hall. There was a fair amount of light, though I couldn't tell its source. A brick stove stood on one side, some broken pots and pans around it. There was a heap of ash in the corner and right in the middle of it was—

Tenida, with his mouth open in shock. And flat on the ground lay the familiar form of Habul Sen.

'Look!' said Tenida, pointing at Habul.

'Habul!' cried Kyabla.

'Why's he lying there like that?' I demanded.

Tenida's voice began to shake. 'They must have murdered him and left his body here!'

I had no idea what was happening to me. All I knew was that terror seemed to be turning me into a terrapin. My arms and legs were trying to curl into my stomach. My back seemed to be freezing into a hard shell. A little longer, and I'd crawl straight into the nearest pond.

I got the words out somehow: 'It's Habul's corpse!'

Tenida unexpectedly burst into tears. 'Oh Habul! How could this happen to you? Must you die before your time? What am I to tell your grandmother in Kolkata? Oh Habul, who's to treat us to alu kabli and Bhimnag's sandesh now?'

'There now, don't cry!' urged Kyabla. 'Let's find out if he's dead or alive first!'

I was close to tears myself. Many were the times Habul had raided his grandmother's storeroom for mango pickles and *kul* preserves and shared the loot with me. The memory sent a pang through my heart. I wiped my nose hastily on the pleats of my dhoti. Crying always gave me a terrible cold in the head.

After three loud sniffs, I managed to say, 'Of course he's dead! Why would he be lying there if he wasn't?'

Kyabla proved the plucky one as usual. Cautiously approaching Habul's corpse, he prodded it in the stomach. To our astonishment, the corpse sat up with a start.

'Baap re, he's turned into a ghost!' Shrieking in terror, I made a wild spring. My head hit Tenida sharply on his battleaxe of a nose. What a rock-hard nose he had! It felt as if someone had drilled a hole through my skull. Tenida set up a yell. 'My nose! My nose!' I sat down heavily on the floor.

In a perfectly good-natured voice and the choicest Dhaka dialect, Habul complained, 'I was sleeping so soundly after all those rasagollas. But you had to come along and spoil it all!'

I felt a sudden twinge of doubt. Spooks were supposed to talk in nasal tones . . . but he was speaking perfectly clear Bengali. In the best Dhaka dialect, too!

'Dear me!' snapped Tenida. 'What lordly ease! Fast asleep, the little nawab, while we wore ourselves out looking for him! Never seen such an idiot.'

Habul yawned luxuriously. 'A grand sleep it was, after that potful of rasagollas! Well, where's Gajada? And the Swamiji?'

'Quite the guest of honour, aren't you?' exclaimed Tenida. 'Swamiji! Gajada!'

'What else?' countered Habul. 'Got here yesterday—and I've been feasting ever since. They've been taking such good care of me—it's like visiting my favourite uncle! Well, where are they?'

'How should we know?' retorted Kyabla. 'How did you fall into their clutches, anyway? And how did you end up here?'

'Why wouldn't I come? A man came up to me and said, "Son, there's treasure hidden inside this mountain. Come along if you want a share." Why lose a chance to be a millionaire? So I came along here. I can't tell you what good care the Swamiji and Gajada have been taking of me!'

Tenida made a face at him. 'Of course you can't! Sitting here gobbling *rajbhog* and driving us out of our wits with worry!'

'We'll talk about that later,' intervened Kyabla. 'How many of them were living in this cave, Habul?'

'About four, I think.'

'What were they doing?'

'How would I know? They had a machine that kept clattering away printing things. I don't see the machine here either! Could they have gone away? What a pity, they kept giving me treats . . .' Habul let out a deep sigh.

'Treats be hanged!' exclaimed Tenida. 'Come on, let's get out of here. We arrived in the nick of time. They'd have fed you to death soon.'

'No, no, they'd have fattened him up, then fried him in cutlets,' I said.

'Don't talk nonsense!' scolded Kyabla. 'Here, Habul, what were they printing?'

'How can I say? It looked like pictures.'

'Pictures!' Kyabla began scratching at his nose. 'In a secret cave in the mountain! Trying to scare away anyone who comes to the bungalow! A blue motor car in the middle of the jungle! Seth Dhunduram!'

'To hell with Seth Dhunduram!' exploded Tenida. 'We've found Habul. Problem solved! That brat might have polished off a potful of rasagollas, but we've got mice singing kirtans in our empty bellies! Come on, let's go.'

'Must we climb that ladder again?' asked I.

'Why the ladder?' said Habul. 'There's a way out right here.'

'Where?'

'Here, right ahead.'

Habul showed us the way. We crossed the long, hall-like tunnel—why, it opened right on to the mountainside! There, close by, was the little stream, and that very sal forest!

'How amazing!' exclaimed Kyabla. 'Why, you could have escaped any time you liked, Habul!'

'Why would I want to escape?' asked Habul, bewildered. 'Such splendid fare! I thought I'd stay a few days and get quite stout and healthy!'

'Stout and healthy!' thundered Tenida. 'Good-for-nothing greedy-guts! It would have served you right if Gajeswar had made cutlets of you after all!'

But no sooner had he spoken than we heard—

The rumble of a motor car!

Where on earth could a motor car have come from? Was it Seth Dhunduram again?

Dhunduram it was. In the same blue car. But it wasn't coming our way. In fact, it was trundling further and further through the forest, till at last it disappeared among the leaves. It could almost have been running away from us in fear.

And in that motor car was a beard fluttering in the breeze. I saw it quite clearly. A white beard stained red with tobacco.

The Great Gloomyswami's beard!

The Bird's Flown

'Tut-tut-tut!' said Kyabla, watching Seth Dhunduram's blue car fade into the distance.

'What's the matter, Kyabla?' asked Tenida.

'What d'you think? *Chiriya bhagalwa!*'

What did that mean?

'Maybe he's offering us *chirey*,' I suggested. 'Where did you find chirey, Kyabla? Do give me some! I'm starving.'

Kyabla screwed up his nose. 'That's enough, you needn't be so clever. Not chirey, you fool—that's rice flakes. "Chiriya bhagalwa" means the bird's flown.'

'Bird? Why, the bird hasn't flown! Don't you see those two crows sitting on that tree?'

'Drat it!' exclaimed Kyabla in exasperation. 'Pela's got nothing in his head but catfish and the juice of basak leaves. Didn't you see them all escaping in Seth Dhunduram's motor car? Didn't you see the Great Gloomyswami's beard?'

'What if they have got away?' demanded Tenida. 'Good riddance!'

Habul had been dozing on his feet. A potful of rasagollas was a powerful soporific. Now he suddenly opened his eyes like an owl teased by daylight. 'Dear, dear, has Gajada gone away? Such a fine fellow!'

'Shut up, Habul, don't talk so much!' Kyabla said severely. 'Gajada a fine fellow? Fine indeed! That's why he wants to scare us away from the bungalow—that's why he sits in a cave in the mountain, secretly printing things! And what can Seth Dhunduram be up to, driving around the jungle in his blue motor car?' He nodded with an air of great wisdom. 'Hmm, hmm, hmm! I've got it!'

'Hmm hmm-ing away very grandly, aren't you?' remarked Tenida. 'Why don't you tell us what you've got?'

Instead of answering his question, Kyabla fixed us with an awful glare. Then he demanded in his sternest tones, 'Who's a coward in our band?'

The way he said it sent a quiver through my sickly spleen. Once, on the day of a maths examination, I had been lying in bed with a tummy ache, pretending to be fast asleep. Mejda was a medical student at the time. Hearing I was ill, he produced an eight-yard-long syringe and said I needed an injection in the stomach. My cramps couldn't disappear quickly enough. Looking at Kyabla made me feel as if he were chasing after me with that very syringe.

I almost blurted out, 'Just me!' but managed to stop myself. 'Who's a coward?' demanded Tenida. 'We're all heroes!'

'Then come on, let's go.'

'Where?'

'We've got to nab that blue motor car.'

What was he saying? Had his brain been fried into fritters? Was he dotty or dyspeptic? Was a motor car like the Great Gloomyswami's beard? Could you just put out your hand and grab it?

Said Habul Sen, 'How will you nab it? Grown wings, have you?'

'Let's make for the main road,' urged Kyabla. 'Lorries go up and down all the time—one of them will pick us up if we offer a little money.'

'And the blue car will be standing there waiting for us, I suppose?'

'Where can it go? To Ramgarh, at the furthest. If we can make it to Ramgarh, we're certain to find them.'

'And what if we don't?' asked I.

'We'll come back again.'

'But what's the point of this wild goose chase?' demanded Tenida. 'Will rushing after them do any good? They're gone, and good riddance! Now we can go back to the bungalow and chew on chicken legs in peace. No fear of hearing that ghastly laughter tonight.'

Kyabla thumped his chest. 'Never! They've fooled us and got away with it—it's enough to give Potoldanga a bad name. There's no living there after this. We'll have to look for houses in Potato-head Lane. It won't do, my friend. If you don't want to come, I'll go on my own. But go I will.'

'Alone?' asked Tenida.

'Alone,' answered Kyabla.

Tenida heaved a deep sigh. 'Come on then, let's set out.'

I gave the top of my head a last scratch. 'But they've got Gajeswar with them. It's true that the scorpion put him off his stride, but if he gets his hands on us this time, he'll make us into cutlets. Or onion curry. Or poppy-seed dumplings.'

'Or catfish curry!' Kyabla stuck out three front teeth at me in a frightful grimace. 'Then you'd better stay here by yourself—we're off.'

Let anyone make fun of catfish curry with potol, and I feel mightily offended. No jokes about that, all right? All Kolkata holds our neighbourhood in awe, and it's called Potoldanga. I have a cousin called Potol who can eat a hundred and fifty potato chops and two hundred brinjal fritters in one sitting. Chhordi had a pet goat called Potol: it ate Mejda's favourite white *nagrai* shoes in exactly seven minutes and thirteen seconds (I timed it with a watch). And need I defend catfish? What other fish is a cat as well? Compared to the rest of the fish kingdom, it's the cat's whiskers. What did those idiots eat? Carp or tiddlers. Carp always reminds me of Panditmoshai carping at me for getting my grammar wrong and rapping me over the head. And tiddlers—pooh, that's what you call children. Tiny little things. Could they compare with catfish?

As I pondered over these mysteries, my ears tingling with indignation, I suddenly noticed the others marching off in a party, leaving me behind.

I had no choice. Abandoning my cogitations on catfish and potol, I hurried after them.

The main road lay about a mile and a half from our bungalow. As we walked along the forest trail, we could see tyre tracks on the ground. At one point, we came upon a sal leaf bag. It was quite new, fresh and crisp. Suddenly curious, I picked it up when the others weren't looking and sniffed at it. Ah! Definitely samosas. The aroma lingered in the bag.

The scoundrels! They'd eaten every crumb. Would it have hurt them to leave one or two?

'Oy Pela—why'd you stop in the middle of the path?' Tenida's bellow rang out.

I was starving. Even the aroma of samosas was a comfort, but they wouldn't let me enjoy it. Hastily dropping the bag, I trudged after them once more. My heart was heavy. I had a deep and secret desire to sniff at that bag some more.

At last we hit the main road. Honk honk! A lorry!

I was about to fling up my hand and cry 'Stop! Stop!' but Kyabla grabbed my arm and hissed, 'Idiot, there's no telling what you'll do next! Can't you see that lorry's heading back from Ramgarh?'

'They might have gone the other way, mightn't they?'

'You're a goat. Don't you see which way the tyre marks turn? It can only mean they've gone to Ramgarh.

Hazaribagh's in the other direction—they haven't gone that way.'

Good god, what a brain Kyabla had! That's why he comes first class in class and gets promotions while all I see are large round zeroes. On my maths paper, especially. I feel noughts should be made more substantial. Why draw circles in pencil on my copybook? Anyone who deserved round noughts should be given a potful of rasagollas. Or at least eight Borobazaar laddus. But not the ones made of sesame seeds—one bite had given me a week's toothache.

Grrr-grunk! A lorry grunted to a halt beside us. It was piled high with wood. Kyabla had waved it down. The driver stuck his head out of the window.

'What is it, young sirs? What are you doing here?'

'You must take us to Ramgarh with you, Driver Saheb!'

'It'll cost you four annas.'

'We'll pay.'

'Hop on, then. But you'll have to sit on the logs.'

'That's all right. We won't mind the logs. Up you get, Tenida! Hop on, Habul! Here, Pela, what are you gaping at? Get on, quick!' Kyabla hustled us on to the lorry.

All very well for the others to leap aboard like frisky young lambs. What about me? By the time I'd been hauled up and deposited atop a pile of timber, a good two inches of tender skin had been scraped off my tummy. I felt raw and red from head to toe.

The lorry lurched into life, honked hoarsely and raced

towards Ramgarh. Ugh—what a beastly juddering! I'd land on my head with a bump any minute. Sprawling across a log, I clasped it to my bosom with both arms.

The lorry sped onwards. And with each bounce and rattle, my scrambled stomach screamed for mercy.

Lethal Laddus and Suspicious Samosas

How that lorry raced along! It seemed to be travelling at the speed of light. On top of that, the logs of wood inside were dancing a drunken reel. Despite being lashed down tightly with lengths of thick rope, they seemed about to burst their bonds and take us flying through the air.

Ever seen ripe jamuns being mashed? They're clapped between a pair of bowls and shaken till the seeds separate from the flesh. My poor spleen was getting the same treatment now. I feared I wouldn't be Pelaram of Potoldanga much longer but a sainted tortoise of Sri Brindaban, squashed into a lump.

And if that wasn't enough, there was a sudden flurry from above. Like the lash of a whip bare inches from my nose. It was a trailing branch.

'Ugh!' said Tenida. 'Kyabla's cleverness will be the end of us.'

That idiot Kyabla was still trying to be funny. 'This isn't

the end,' he said, 'just the middle of the road. The road to Ramgarh, to be precise.'

'The middle of the road!' Tenida ground his teeth. 'Just you wait till we get to Ramgarh . . .'

The sentence broke off short in a horrible gulping noise. But Tenida wasn't actually threatening to eat Kyabla at the end of the ride. The gulp had just been shaken out of him by a particularly hard bounce.

Habul began to whine. 'That's done it,' he moaned. 'Gajada's rasagollas are churning into cottage cheese in my stomach.'

'Cottage cheese?' said I. 'Wait till they melt into milk.'

Now Tenida joined in. 'Milk? Why, milk won't be the end of it. Wait till entire cows start butting out of our bellies—horns, hooves and all.'

'You're right,' moaned Habul. 'We'll have a whole dairy soon.'

Kyabla suddenly carolled:

When you lost yourself in trance
And danced your world-destroying dance,
Great Nataraj—

An outraged Tenida was about to yell at him when all our bones were rattled by another fit of jolting. 'Grr-grr-grunt,' said Tenida succinctly.

But all bad things, like good ones, come to an end. At last the lorry rattled into Ramgarh Bazaar. It was moving more slowly now and we were just managing to sit upright on the logs, when suddenly—

'*Arey* Bhaglu, look at that, brother! Four monkeys on a lorry!'

Three urchins grinned toothily up at us.

I lost my temper. 'Monkeys yourselves! Idiots!'

At that, one of the youths aimed a stone at me, narrowly missing my ear. 'I'll pull the pigtails from your heads!' yelled the lorry driver.

Actually, none of the boys had a pigtail but they vanished promptly, pulling faces at us as they went.

The lorry had gone only a little further when Kyabla suddenly exclaimed, 'Look, Tenida, quick! There's the blue car!'

We looked—and there it was. Seth Dhunduram's blue motor car stood outside a sweet shop some distance ahead of us.

My heart began to thump inside my chest. Gajeswar again! That almighty ox of a man! Why, we were better off turning turtle in a jolting lorry. Facing Gajeswar would be far more painful.

But Kyabla wouldn't give up. He finally succeeded in dragging us off the lorry.

'Listen, Pela! Sit under this peepul tree with Habul and watch the car. Tenida and I have another little job to do.'

The lorry driver had got his four annas and driven off. If the lorry had been at hand, I'd have hopped on and gone wherever it took me. A nice fix I was in. Sit under the peepul tree watching Seth Dhunduram's car! Get my neck wrung by Gajeswar Garui, more likely.

'Why don't I go with you?' I suggested, scratching my nose thoughtfully. 'I'm sure Habul can manage by himself here.'

'Don't act clever,' admonished Kyabla. 'Do as I tell you— sit here and stay put. And don't take your eyes off that car. We'll be back in ten minutes. Come on, Tenida.'

With that, the two of them vanished down the next alley.

I said, 'Habul?'

'Hmm?'

'Did you see that?'

Habul had now sat down at the base of the tree. With a huge yawn, he said, 'Hmm, you're right.'

'Does it make any sense, sitting here like idiots?'

Habul yawned again. 'Hmm no. Sleeping's better. I'd just nodded off when you lot woke me up and threw me into that jolting lorry! Ugh, I feel sick!'

So saying, he leaned back against the trunk. His eyes closed at once. And believe it or not, within the next few seconds he was snoring gently.

Just imagine!

'Habul! Hey Habul!' I called.

Habul stopped snoring. 'Uh?' he said inquiringly.

'How can you sleep like this, under a tree in broad daylight?'

'Now shut up, Pela,' said Habul aggrievedly. 'Stop squawking, I tell you! Let me sleep in peace.' And in a minute he was asleep again, very peacefully. Gentle little snores fluttered from his nostrils, like a flock of sparrows from their nest.

What a villain! What a low villain! Was I to watch the car by myself now? An unspeakable rage boiled up in me. So did a keen desire to clip him on the ear. I realized, however, that I could do better. An army of fat red ants was just marching by. Why not let a few loose on Habul's nose?

I was just about to scoop up some ants in a dry leaf when all of a sudden—

'Arey khonka! You are being here?'

I looked up and beheld the familiar bulk of Seth Dhunduram.

A dozen potol wriggled and a good two dozen catfish jumped in my stomach in fright. My mouth fell open. All I could say was, 'Uh—uh—uh—'

Seth Dhunduram smiled. 'You are coming to visit Ramgarh? Good, very good. But why sitting under this tree? Your face telling me you are being very hungry.'

Hungry? Did the man know what he was saying? Just sniffing at that sal leaf packet had soured my mood for the rest of the expedition. I could have eaten heaven and the pits of hell. I would have willingly taken a bite out of Dhunduram's superb paunch. But how could I admit such a thing?

Seth Dhunduram said cajolingly, 'Arey, you are being hungry—why so ashamed? Come with me. In that shop you are getting excellent laddus—also hot samosas! You liking to eat? Myself treating—you not paying!'

Bears and tigers can't daunt Pelaram of Potoldanga. His chest swells, and he stands erect in the face of Tenida's

109

almighty cuffs. A zero in the maths exam leaves him unmoved. But talk of food and you've vanquished our hero forever.

I objected feebly, 'But Sethji, Gajeswar—'

Dhunduram rolled his eyes. 'Gajeswar? Which Gajeswar?'

'Why, that huge strong man—the one who looks like an elephant—the one with you in your car.'

'Ram, Ram, Sitaram!' exclaimed the Sethji piously. 'I am knowing no such Gajeswar! And no one but myself being in my car!'

'But the beard of the Great Gloomyswami—'

'Gloomyswami?' The Sethji looked thoughtful. 'Yes, yes, an old man be getting into the car on the way. He telling me, "Sethji, I be getting down at Ramgarh Bazaar." So I be dropping him there. He be going off to the station.'

What doubts could I have after this?

Dhunduram said again, 'Come, khonka, come. Excellent laddus here—hot samosas too.'

There was no resisting him. Pelaram of Potoldanga admitted defeat. Habul was still snoring, the little sparrows flitting gaily from his nostrils. I toyed with the idea of waking him, but thought better of it. Then I scuttled along after Dhunduram myself.

It was a huge sweet shop. Row on row of laddus and *motichur*. Hot samosas sizzling in an enormous cauldron. The scent was enough to drive me wild.

'Come, khonka. Come in!' invited the Sethji.

I peered in. Not a glimpse of Gajeswar or the Gloomyswami's sacred pigtail.

In I went.

At the back of the shop was a small eating room. The Sethji sat down and placed a prompt order. 'A dozen of the special laddus and six samosas–'

I objected modestly. 'Why so much, Sethji?'

'Eat, child, eat. Very good they are being,' said the Sethji benignly.

The very good things arrived on a sal leaf platter. I tasted a laddu—why, it was like nectar! And were those samosas or fresh catfish-curry with tender potol? I needed no more encouragement, but fell to work.

I had eaten four laddus and two samosas when my head began to spin. Everything grew dark before my eyes. And then—

I heard it loud and clear—Gajeswar Garui's laugh.

'Got him! A real little pest he is too. I'll make alu kabli out of him this very day!'

That did it. Utter blackness engulfed my world. I toppled over, chair and all, and fell unconscious to the floor.

The Game Ends

When I regained my senses, my first thought was, 'Where am I?'

And where was the Jhantipahari bungalow? Where was Ramgarh? Where was anything? Looking around me, I could hardly believe my eyes.

I found myself perched atop a huge mountain. Not quite on the peak perhaps, but a little lower. The summit glowed like the mouth of a furnace, licked by fiery tongues.

I had read about them in my geography book, I had seen them in films. I knew right away what sort of mountain this was. 'It's a volcano!' I blurted out.

Loud guffaws rang out as soon as I'd spoken. What a burst of laughter! The whole mountain seemed to quiver with the sound. A huge spire of flame shot out of the volcano and leapt into the sky.

I looked around and saw three men sitting close by, laughing their heads off. One of them was Seth

Dhunduram, his giant belly rippling to the rhythm of rich chuckles. Beside him was the Great Gloomyswami, tugging at his own beard in his mirth. The ogre-like Gajeswar stood leaning against the hillside. The grin on his face would have swallowed the heavens, and he shook with thunderous laughter.

On seeing these three, my pure young soul flew like a bird from its mortal cage. An earthquake seemed to seize my sickly spleen.

'Why're you laughing?' I spluttered in shock. 'What's so funny?'

More laughter greeted this question. Gajeswar sat down abruptly, gripping his stomach.

'Ho ho,' chortled Seth Dhunduram. 'A volcano it is being! Do you know which volcano, khonka?'

'How should I know? I've never seen it before!'

'It is being Vesuvius!'

'Vesuvius!' I goggled at him. Why, I'd been in Ramgarh all this while with no idea that it was just a stone's throw from Vesuvius.

'But Vesuvius is in Germany,' I objected. 'Or is it Africa?'

Gajeswar rolled his eyes and grimaced frightfully at me.

'Knows a lot, doesn't he? And he hopes to pass the school finals with those brains! Vesuvius in Germany! Vesuvius in Africa! Pah!'

I scratched my nose. 'It must be in America then?' I suggested.

'Ugh, it's not even cow dung that you've got for brains,' shuddered Gajeswar. 'It's dry dung cakes. You don't get those noughts in your exams for nothing. Vesuvius is in Italy.'

'Well, possibly. But Italy or America, it's all the same.'

'All the same?' scowled Gajeswar. 'Are your face and your foot the same? Is mutton curry the same as *polta* leaf dumplings?'

The Great Gloomyswami sneered, 'Let him be! His head's worth no more than his hide. Nothing in it but fresh potol and catfish curry.'

It always infuriates me when people make fun of catfish curry with potol. 'What's that to you?' I snapped. 'The question is, how did I get to Italy from Ramgarh? And when? What's happened to Tenida, Habul Sen and Kyabla? I can't see a single one of them!'

'Nor will you.' Gajeswar smiled slyly. 'I've digested them.'

'Digested them! What d'you mean?'

'What d'you think I mean? They're in my stomach. I've eaten the whole lot.'

'Eaten them!' The spleen in my own stomach did a reckless high jump. 'Are you serious?'

The trio burst into horrible laughter once more. The noise brought tongues of flame leaping out of Vesuvius' fiery mouth. I pressed both hands to my ears.

When he had finally stopped laughing, the Great Gloomyswami said, 'Trying to outsmart us, son? Why, you're a tiddler fighting a tomcat! A goat kicking at a Royal Bengal tiger! By the power of my spells, I had the four of you here in a trice. And then—'

'We roasted Habul Sen—' struck in the Sethji.

'We made cutlets of your leader Tenida—' growled Gajeswar.

'We fried that frisky young Kyabla,' said the Gloomyswami meditatively.

'And then we ate them,' concluded the Sethji.

My bottlebrush hair stood bolt upright on my head. I gulped several times and said, 'Yikes.'

'Now it's your turn,' said the Swamiji.

'Yikes!'

'Enough "Yikes" from you. You'll know what we mean in a second. Gajeswar!' thundered the Gloomyswami.

With folded hands Gajeswar answered, 'Yes, Maharaj.'

'Put the pot on.'

No sooner had he spoken than Gajeswar produced a huge cauldron. What a vessel! It looked like a small boat. You could have curried all the four heroes of Potolodanga in it at once.

'Put it on the fire,' commanded Gloomyswami. Gajeswar hurried up to the top of Vesuvius. Then, just as you'd set a pot on a clay oven, he placed that enormous cauldron right over the volcano's bubbling mouth.

'Do we have enough oil?' inquired the Swamiji.

'Yes, Maharaj,' replied Gajeswar.

'Pure oil?'

'From my own oil press it is coming, Maharaj,' Seth Dhunduram assured him. 'Pure as oil can be. Not a drop is diluted.'

'That's all right then,' said the Great Gloomyswami, stroking his beard. 'Diluted oil doesn't do the trick, and gives me acidity besides.'

I could bear it no longer. 'What are you going to do with pure oil?' I wailed.

'Fry you,' said Gajeswar Garui shortly.

'Then, with plenty of crisp hot puffed rice—' began the Swamiji.

'We'll crunch you up,' finished Seth Dhunduram.

That was it, then. Pelaram of Potoldanga was definitely a goner. His time had come. No longer would tender potol or catfish be bought for him at the Sealdah market. He'd vanish into the bellies of these three ogres, unwept and unsung.

All of a sudden, I felt curiously detached from the situation, calm and meditative. Do you know how it seemed? Imagine you're sitting down to a maths exam. Looking at the paper, you realize you can't solve a single sum—none of them make sense to you. You work yourself into a sweat over the first one. Your head grows hot, your ears buzz like crickets, a dragonfly hops up and down on the end of your nose. Then, very slowly, a deep peace spreads over your soul. You embellish your answer book with a sketch of a coconut tree. Hills rise behind it, a moon appears above, a flock of birds decide to fly across the page, and so on. In other words, having abandoned all hope of passing in maths, you're inspired to become an artist.

So it was with me now. When I realized all hope was gone, a musical fit came over me. Even if I was doomed, I could at least sing to my heart's desire. I'd never been allowed to sing at home. Whenever I tried, Mejda came chasing after me with his fat medical textbooks. I'd let out a few notes on the Chatterjees' terrace, but Tenida put a stop to that with a smart rap across my head. I'd sing my swansong here. It would be the first—and last—song I ever sang.

'Master! Swamiji!' I appealed.

'Tell us what you want,' invited the Swamiji. 'Which would you prefer—to be coated in *besan* or just dipped in salt and turmeric?'

'Fry me any way you like,' I said. 'I don't mind. I have just one request. I'd like to sing awhile. It'll be my last song before I die.'

'That's not a bad idea, Master,' grunted Gajeswar. 'A little music before a meal is always welcome. The tribes of Africa dance and sing before they roast their victims. Strike up, lad . . .'

'Yes, yes, a nice song—sing it with feeling,' urged Seth Dhunduram.

I closed my eyes and began:

Once upon a time a wolf
Was cast into despair
A sharp fishbone got in his throat
And lodged securely there—

'What sort of song is this being!' expostulated the Sethji. 'It's a fable from the *Kathamala*!'

'No, no,' said the Swamiji. 'It's quite expressive. What a sweet tune! And what a splendid screech owl's voice! Sing on, boy, sing on!'

I went on, my eyes still shut:

His throat grew sore, his voice was hoarse
Why, he could hardly talk
Tears came into his eyes and he
Went sobbing to a stork—

I had got this far when I heard the tinkling of anklets. It sounded as if someone was dancing. I opened my eyes and saw . . .

Gajeswar dancing.

Gajeswar, none else. Heaven knows when he had managed to put on a *ghagra*, hook on a nose ring and tie a pair of anklets on his feet. Now he was pirouetting about like a peacock. What a dance it was! I don't know if the demoness Taraka ever found occasion to dance ghagra-clad in the Ramayana, but if she did, I swear she'd be no match for Gajeswar. Seeing me gaping at him, Gajeswar smiled coyly.

'What are you gawping at, eh? I say, what are you staring at? Can your Uday Shankars dance like this? Pooh! It's pure Kathakali I'm performing here!'

'You could call it Manipuri, even,' commented the Swamiji.

'Yes, yes, or Kathak you could be calling it,' the Sethji mused.

'You could call it Taraka-dancing too,' I suggested.

'What's that?' demanded Gajeswar.

I checked myself hastily. 'Nothing, nothing, nothing important.'

'It had better not be,' Gajeswar flounced his skirt and twirled around once more. 'But why have you stopped singing? Pipe up! I'll have one good dance before you go.'

Sing? The sight of Gajeswar dancing had scrambled all the songs in my head into semolina pudding.

'Tcha tcha,' he rebuked. 'Is this all you're good for? You can't sing to save your life. Now listen—I'll sing you a real classical piece as I dance.'

So saying, he burst into song:

Now Kali, I'll stew and eat you
Eat you in a hurry
Snatch away your string of skulls
And cook them into curry . . .

With that, he danced. How he danced! It was as if Vesuvius itself were dancing with him. Swamiji closed his eyes and began waggling his head to the rhythm of his steps, the Sethji exclaimed, 'Ah! How delightful is the dancing! My heart—it is filling with joy!'

Well it might, given how entranced he and the swami were by Gajeswar's performance. From deep inside my malarial spleen, a voice spoke to me. It said, 'Pelaram of Potoldanga, this is it. Your last chance. If you want to escape—'

Right.

Do or die. I would make one last bid for freedom.

I got to my feet. Then I ran for my life.

But was it so easy to escape from the summit of Vesuvius? I hadn't taken three steps when I skidded on some loose pebbles and landed flat on my face.

And instantly—

Gajeswar's dance stopped. Longer than twenty ordinary arms, his arm shot down from the top of the mountain. 'Clever, aren't you?' he said. 'Thinking of sneaking off while I was dancing? See what happens to you now!' That arm, so like an elephant's trunk, fastened around my throat and began to swing me back and forth through the air. 'Glory to the Great Gloomyswami!' Gajeswar's yell shook the heavens. And then—splash! Into that great cauldron of boiling oil . . .

No, it wasn't boiling oil after all. In fact, it was a lot of cold water. I started up, gasping for breath. Nothing seemed to be making much sense. Misty figures floated before my eyes—Vesuvius, Gajeswar dancing in a ghagra, that enormous pot full of bubbling oil.

'They must have drugged him,' said a grave voice.

I looked in its direction and saw it belonged to the police inspector standing there stroking his moustache. With him were six or seven policemen and—with ropes around their waists—the Great Gloomyswami, Seth Dhunduram and the almighty Gajeswar!

Tenida was pouring water over my head. Habul was fanning me. And Kyabla was saying, 'Get up, Pela, get up! We went straight to the nearest police station and the police came and arrested the lot of them. They were forging banknotes in their den just below the Jhantipahari bungalow. Swamiji's their leader. Seth Dhunduram used to circulate the fake notes. We've seized all they had, even the machine on which the notes were printed. We found everything stashed in their car. D'you understand, you nitwit? No fear of ghosts in the Jhantipahari bungalow after this!'

The inspector smiled. 'Well done, lads; you're a brave lot. This is a fine thing you've managed to do. We've been trying to get our hands on these three for a long time, but could never track them down. We've nabbed them today, all because of you. You'll get good money for this. The government will reward you.'

Could one sit still after this? For even a second? I, Pelaram of Potoldanga, leapt up at once and yelled, 'Potoldanga—'

Tenida, Habul Sen and Kyabla shouted in chorus, 'Forever!'

SHORT STORIES

The Bhajahari Film Corporation

Walking through Bowbazaar, Tenida suddenly stopped in front of Bhim Nag's sweet shop. He wouldn't budge from the spot. 'Why're you standing in the middle of the street?' I asked. 'Come on.'

'Go on? Go on? Must we really go on?' Tenida looked at me pleadingly. 'Pela, is that heart of yours solid stone? Just look, row upon row of *sandesh*, platters of golden rajbhog beckoning to us, rasagollas and *gulab jamuns* swimming in syrup . . . Pela, my friend . . .'

I shook my head. 'You're not fooling me. At present, I have exactly three rupees in my pocket, and I have to buy Uncle his Ayurvedic medicine. We're getting late, so come on.'

'I'm really very hungry,' Tenida noisily sucked in some drool. 'What if you loan me a couple of rupees now, and I get Uncle's medicine in the evening?'

But Pelaram Banerjee wasn't about to fall for that one. The almighty being who manages to get Tenida to return a loan has yet to grace the world. I put my hand firmly over my pocket and said, 'I've no sympathy for the way your stomach starts growling the moment you catch sight of a food shop. Besides, if I don't get Uncle's medicine to him by the end of the morning, who's going to sew my ear back on my head again? You?'

Tenida heaved a sigh like the rumble of a railway engine.

'You've cast a Brahmin into affliction, Pela, and that, too, in the morning—you'll go to hell when you die.'

'I'll risk it. I know Uncle's ear-twisting—beats hell any day. And you're some Brahmin! Haven't I seen you chewing on chicken drumsticks at Dilkhosh Restaurant?'

'It's a false world.' Tenida turned his eyes to feast on Bhim Nag's sweets one last time. 'No, you can't be happy till you're rich.'

Our evening chat on the Chatterjees' front step continued along the same lines. Kyabla had gone to the zoo with his uncle; Habul Sen was having a tooth extracted. So it was just the two of us. A despondent Tenida had consumed two bags full of fries. I had paid for them, and my share had ended at half a potato fritter.

Tenida wiped his mouth on the sleeve of my kurta. Then he said, 'You see Pela, there's really no getting along any more unless you're rich.'

'So get rich,' I said encouragingly.

'Get rich, he says—as if it's very easy! Who'll put up the money? Will you?' Tenida made a face at me. I shook my head to say I wouldn't.

'Well then?'

'Buy a lottery ticket,' I advised.

'Damn your lottery tickets! I'm tired of buying them, and I've yet to see a penny. All I got out of it was a couple of thumping slaps from Borda when I stole the grocery money to pay for them. The lottery's no good. We need a business.'

'A business!'

'Yes, a business.' Tenida's face grew grave with the weight of his plan. 'You know what the ancient books say. "One must engage in trade—it means the blessing of Lakshmi." It's the only road for us, understand?'

'Yes, I do. But you need money for that, too!'

'We won't need a paisa of our own for the one we'll start. We'll use the wealth of others . . . by playing a little trick on them.'

'What kind of business is that?' I asked, bemused.

'Hmm, let's hear you guess?' Tenida screwed up his eyes and smiled a little smile. 'Can't think of it, can you? It's not the work of empty heads like yours. You need a real brain for it, see?' He proudly rapped his own crown twice.

'Why're you teasing me?' I said humbly. 'Spill the beans.'

Tenida looked around suspiciously for eavesdroppers and then placed his lips to my ear. 'A film company,' he whispered.

'What?' I leapt up.

'Stop braying like a donkey!' bellowed Tenida. 'I've planned the whole thing to perfection. You'll write the stories; I'll direct them. You'll see, it'll be a sensation!'

'What do you know about films?' I enquired.

'Who knows anything about films?' Tenida looked contemptuous. 'Everyone's the same. They've all got cow dung in their heads. Three fights, eight songs, a few fake buildings and you've got a film. Why, I've been to Tollygunge to watch one being shot.'

'But still—'

'Hang it, you're a dolt—' said Tenida, annoyed. 'D'you think we're really going to film anything? Who wants all that trouble?'

'Then?'

'We'll sell shares in it. If we can sell off a good few—d'you get it?' Tenida winked. 'Dwarik's, Bhim Nag's, Dilkhosh, K.C. Das—'

At this, my mouth began to water. I gulped. 'Enough, enough, you needn't go on.'

The next day, the entire neighbourhood was awash with posters.

The Bhajahari Film Corporation
It's coming! It's coming!
The Thrilling Saga
The Horror!
Direction: Bhajahari Mukhopadhyay (Tenida)
Story: Pelaram Bandyopadhyay

Beneath, in smaller lettering:

The public are invited to buy shares. Each share is available at the modest sum of eight annas. Three shares are offered at just one rupee.

Below this, a drawing of a hand, and the words:

Special attraction! Shareholders win chances to act. Do not neglect this golden opportunity! Shares limited—buy immediately, or regret later. Enquire at – No. 18, Potoldanga Street, Kolkata.

A few hours and we had first-hand proof of the effects of a good ad. In fact, the evidence was so strong that we barely survived it. We'd never hoped the idea would catch on so quickly. Tenida's huge house stood quite empty at the time; the family had gone off to Deoghar for a change of air. Tenida, whose Matriculation Exam was approaching, had remained at home with a servant, Bishtu. The two of us were sitting comfortably in his room on the second floor, listening to the radio and guzzling mutton *ghugni*. Suddenly, Bishtu arrived, every inch the messenger carrying news of defeat in battle.

Bishtu's home is in Chittagong. His nasal babbling isn't easy to understand; still, what we did make of his message filled us with alarm. Tenida choked violently on his ghugni.

Bishtu informed us, 'The 'ounse 'ans 'een 'ancked by onbbers.' (The house has been attacked by robbers.)

What was the scamp saying! Was he batty or bilious? A coon or a codfish? Robbers attacking a house in the heart of Kolkata, in the middle of the afternoon!

'Um ownstairs an ee or younrelves (Come downstairs and see for yourselves),' Bishtu continued, pale-faced.

I was considering a retreat to safety under the bed, but Tenida let out a tiger's roar that jogged my sickly spleen.

'Coward! Come along, march! I'll flatten the villain's nose with one good punch!'

Now, as for me, pathetic Pelaram Banerjee, holding body and soul together with a little light catfish curry, I don't enjoy these exciting encounters with robbers. There we were, quite happy, did we need all this fuss?

I tried to escape—'Um, you see, I'm beginning to get such a stomach ache . . .'

'Stomach ache!' bellowed Tenida. 'Why, you seemed to have forgotten all about it while you were polishing off that mutton ghugni! Now come along, Pela, or you'll be the first one I—'

Tenida left his sentence unfinished, but I got his meaning at once.

'Praise to Goddess Durga . . .' I followed him tremblingly.

But no, it wasn't robbers. A queue stretched from Potoldanga to College Street!

Had anyone stayed away? There were schoolboys, the cigarette-seller from the street corner, the maid from next door, an Oriya cook and even two awe-inspiring giants of kabuliwallahs, as menacing as Yama's messengers.

As soon as we appeared, the crowd erupted into yells.

'I want to buy some shares!'

'Here you are, Sir, eight annas!'

The maid declared, 'Look sons, I've brought a whole rupee. Give me three shares—and a chance to play the heroine!'

The Oriya cook from the boarding house next door struck in: 'I've brought eight annas as well . . .'

Over the rest of the din came the two kabuliwallahs' rough tones: 'O Babu, we've brought a rupee each, we want chances too . . .'

And there rose a chorus of screams: 'A chance! A chance!' It made my head spin—clapping my hands over my ears, I sank to the ground.

Tenida the Incredible kept remained standing. Standing calm and quiet, Buddha-like. As if that wasn't enough, I saw a flash of teeth stretching from ear to ear—he was all smiles.

Then he declared, 'Yes, yes, you'll have your chances—' stretching his hand out in a reassuring gesture—'everyone will get a chance. Now let's see you precious lot fork out your cash. I'm warning you, don't try and palm off any dud coins on us, or else—'

'Jai Hind . . . Jai Hind . . .'

When the crowd had dispersed, Tenida flung both hands above his head and broke into a jig. Then he sat down heavily, and landed flat on his back on the floor, complete with his chair.

I exclaimed in protest.

But Tenida was already on his feet. Then he thumped my back so enthusiastically that I yelled. 'O Pela, today's a great day, no day for tears! The game is ours! Bhim Nag, Dwarik Ghosh, Chacha's Hotel, Dilkhosh . . . ahh!'

Forgetting my agony, I echoed, 'Ahh!'

'Come on, let's count it all up'. He grinned from ear to ear again.

Our earnings were quite respectable—twenty-six rupees and twelve annas.

'Twelve annas?' Tenida frowned. 'How could it come to twelve annas? If the rates were eight annas and a rupee . . . uh-huh—some rascal must have cheated us out of four annas in all that confusion . . . what d'you think?'

I nodded in agreement.

'They're all rogues in this world. Why can't you find a single honest man? Cheating a Brahmin out of four whole annas, that, too, first thing in the morning,' Tenida sighed. 'Never mind, what we've got isn't bad. Dilkhosh, Bhim Nag, Dwarik Ghosh . . .'

I continued the chant: 'Chacha's Hotel, K.C. Das . . .'

'Etcetera, etcetera,' concluded Tenida. 'But look here, Pela, I'll tell you something right away. The plan was mine from start to finish. The profits, son, will be split accordingly. Fourteen annas to two annas.'

'How can that be?' I protested.

Tenida landed a ferocious rap on the table, 'Yes, that's how it is. And if not, how will it be if I throw you straight out of the first-floor window?'

I scratched my ear and agreed that it wouldn't be good.

'Then come along, let's celebrate Bhajahari Film Corporation's first project with some Mughlai parathas and a few plates of chicken curry.'

Tenida burst into a room-splitting roar of diabolical laughter. The noise brought Bishtu scurrying out. He stood gaping for a while, then commented, 'Chhontobabu must 'anve gone noff 'is 'ead.'

A few days passed happily. We were growing quite fat on rajbhog from Darik's and cutlets from Chacha's. As we demolished K.C. Das's *rasamalais*, we wondered if we could hatch another plan, when suddenly—

It was like a clap of thunder on our threshold. There stood those two giant kabuliwallahs, bloodlust bubbling from the innards of those massive robes, those heavy beards.

As soon as we turned towards them, they thumped their cudgels. 'O Babu, where's our money, eh? And what about our chances?'

'What?' The rasamalai slipped from Tenida's hand into his breast pocket. 'Pela, we're done for!'

'Of course we are!' I retorted. 'But I've the advantage of you this time. Fourteen annas' worth of pounding for you ... that's to say, they'll beat you to pulp. On the other hand, I might just survive my two annas' worth.'

The kabuliwallahs called again, 'O Bhojohori Babu, come on out . . .'

Going out would mean direct passage to the Nimtala cremation grounds. Tenida jumped up, then clamped me under his arm and dragged me through a side door in a different direction.

'Well then, you sons of honest men, where's my money and my chance?' There stood the maid, gripping the blade she used to scale fish with.

'What about my chance?' demanded the Oriya cook, dangerously swinging a rice ladle.

'Think you'll get away with your swindle, Sir? We're Shyambazar boys!' a group of youths rolled up their sleeves and charged at us.

For a moment, the world spun dizzily before my eyes. Then I heard a shout of 'Do or die!' And hoisting me on to his shoulder, Tenida leapt forward.

I was only dimly conscious of what followed. I could make out a ghastly din—'Thief! Thief! He's getting away!'— and through it all, a sensation of flight, as if I was whooshing along on the Punjab Mail.

Hitting the ground with a thud, I cried out. When I opened my eyes, I found myself at Howrah Station. Tenida was panting exactly like a railway engine.

'Huh,' he said, 'as if those louts could catch me! I'm champion of the five-hundred-metre race. Now off you go, Pela. I've still got twelve rupees and four annas in my pocket, so quick, get two tickets for Deoghar. The Delhi Express is about to leave.'

The Little Bat and the Ticket-Checker

'So you see, Pela, little bats are very dangerous.'

Potoldanga's Tenida was eating ghugni out of a torn sal leaf. Some of the gravy trickled through a hole in the bottom; Tenida licked it up in a flash, crumpled the leaf into a ball and threw it straight at Kyabla's nose. Then he repeated, 'Yes, yes, very dangerous, those little bats.'

'How do you know that?' Habul Sen's Dhaka tone held a note of challenge.

'Well then, tell me the English word for *chamchikey*.'

Kyabla, Habul Sen and I looked helplessly at each other's faces.

In the end, after much meditation, Kyabla ventured, 'Small bat. A chamchikey is a small bat, isn't it?'

'Idiot!'

'Then it must be batlet,' I said. 'No? What, then? Bat's son? No? In that case, what do you call a brickbat?'

'Shut up, you gibbon,' snarled Tenida. 'A brickbat's a brick. Of the kind I'll break over your head soon.'

Habul Sen declared, with a grave face, 'Got it.'

'Got what?'

'Skin mole.'

'Skin mole?' Tenida's nose, curved like a battleaxe, now reared up like a monument. 'What on earth is that?'

'Skin for the first part of chamchikey: *cham,* or *chamra.* And in our part of Bengal they call a mole a *chika.* Join the two and you get skin mole.'

Tenida lost his temper: 'Look here, Habul, there's a limit to jokes. Skin mole, indeed! What a linguist you are!'

I asked, 'Well, why're you quizzing us on translations of chamchikey? Go and look it up in the dictionary!'

'Not even the dictionary has it,' said Tenida, with a triumphant chuckle.

'So what?'

'That proves what a dangerous creature a chamchikey is. It means it's so terrible that even the British are afraid of it. Just think—people who hunt lions and gorillas in the jungles of Africa, people who let off bombs and cannons in wars—they're too scared to even speak of the chamchikey. Why, I've seen the fuss they make with my own eyes.'

'What fuss?' The scent of a story made us pounce on Tenida. 'Tell us at once.'

'In that case, Kyabla, scoot! Get two more annas' worth of mutton ghugni from the shop at the corner of the lane. No story without fodder.'

With a long face, Kyabla departed to fetch the ghugni. Tenida polished it off, not leaving a single morsel for us. Then he began: 'Now listen . . .'

'I had gone to visit my uncle in Patna. He works in the railways, so when I was to return, he put me on the Delhi Express without a ticket and said, "My friend Chatterjee's in charge of the train. Don't worry, he'll see you safely through to Howrah Station."

'So I felt quite confident as I got into an empty second-class compartment and stretched out on a bunk. It was a winter night, and it gets really cold in western India. I was chilled to the bone.

'But who was to know that on that very night, halfway through the journey, Chatterjee was to exchange duties with an Englishman, Mr—what's his name—Rhinoceros.'

Kyabla interrupted, 'A rhinoceros is a fierce animal.'

'Shut up, show off!' Tenida ground his teeth, 'little dictionary! What's it to you if the parents of that Englishman had named their son after a fierce animal? Hasn't your name changed from Kishalay Kumar to Kyabla? What harm has it done?'

'Let him be,' intervened Habul Sen. 'He's only a kid.'

'Kid! If he opens his mouth again, I'll make cutlets out of him. Anyway, listen to what happened. I had shut all the doors and windows tight and lain down. But I just couldn't sleep. For one thing, not even two blankets could keep the cold out. For another, I'd eaten far too much at dinner. The goat cooked at my uncle's house seemed to have come to life inside me. It was butting the wall of my stomach to the rhythm of the carriage wheels. I shouldn't have been so greedy.

'You know how indigestion gives one strange dreams. I dreamt that the demon Vatapi—no, Ilbal—well, one of the two—had entered my stomach in the shape of a goat. And an ogre was saying in Hindi, "Hey Ilbal, now blow his stomach open and come out—"

'"Help!" I yelled.

'Opening my eyes, I found neither Vatapi nor Ilbal in the carriage—there was only a little bat fluttering around. Once it sped straight past my face—nearly gripped my nose with its claws.

'I was in a nice fix!

'Who knows how it had got in? All the doors and windows around me were shut. But with a chamchikey anything's possible. Nothing's beyond a little bat . . .

'I thought of getting up and driving it out. But it was too cold . . . who'd stir out of those blankets? Besides, if I tried to get up, the goat in my stomach would probably burst out of it, horns and all. But then the bat skimmed past my nose again, nearly settling on the tip. Perhaps it mistook my long, steep stretch of nose for a real monument.

'I pulled a frightful grimace and said "Phoorr . . . phoosh!" I thought that would scare it away. Perhaps it did get a fright. At any rate, it whizzed off and suspended itself from a coat hanger, dangling from it like a tiny black bundle. Just then, the door to my compartment rattled noisily.

'Who could have come to disturb me at this time of night? I was sure it was some other passenger. At first I thought of lying low. Let him rattle to his heart's content and then go away. I buried my face in the blankets.

'But the train had stopped at some godforsaken station. There it stood, as if it had been invited to dinner! Meanwhile, the rattling continued, fit to break down the door.

'What an idiot! Were there no other compartments on the train? Was he obsessed with this one? I felt quite furious. But I had to open the door . . . after all, it wasn't a reserved carriage. Vowing to abuse him in choice Hindi and in my sternest voice, I got up.'

Kyabla interrupted suddenly, 'Tenida, you don't know any Hindi at all.'

'What d'you mean?'

'What you say never makes sense in Hindi. I've lived in the western parts since my childhood—'

'Shut up, I tell you, Kyabla!' Tenida roared. 'If you contradict me one more time, I'll turn you into pudding with a single punch. Even our cook ran away to Chhapra district when he heard me speak Hindi!'

'Never mind,' soothed Habul. 'What does it matter what that little shrimp says?'

'Shrimp! I'll fry him in oil and eat him up!'

'Oh, he's completely inedible,' I pointed out. 'He'll give you stomach ache and indigestion. You'd better finish the story.'

'All right, listen.' Having silenced Kyabla, Tenida went on.

'I had got up, and was just about to open the door and demand, in Hindi, "What kind of a fellow are you, eh?" when I heard a ferocious grunting.'

'Grunting?'

'The Englishman. The ticket checker.'

'You mean Rhinoceros?' Kyabla blurted out despite Tenida's scolding.

'Who else? A real sahib from head to toe. Skin as fair as if it had been whitewashed, face like a rice pot, huge nostrils bristling with stiff red hairs, a smile revealing teeth like huge radishes, a voice like a bull's bellow—the real thing! No sooner had he entered than he addressed me in flawless English: "Fast asleep so early in the evening? It's the worst habit possible."'

'What sort of flawless English, Tenida?' I wanted to know.

'Why do you care?' said Tenida with a contemptuous laugh. 'You wouldn't understand it if I told you—it's a sahib's English, after all! Never mind. I was stunned by his words. Calling midnight early evening? What do they call night, in that case? Morning?

'The next thing he said was, "Where's your ticket?"

'I had my answer ready. I said, "I'm the nephew of Mr Banerjee of Patna. He's told the head of the train's staff, Mr Chatterjee, about me."

'On hearing this, the Sahib bared his teeth at me like a radish seller showing off his stock. A storm blew up in the hairs lining his nostrils, and he let out a low growl.

What he said next made my eyes grow round with shock.

"'I don't give a damn about your uncle Banerjee! All you WTs make up uncles of that sort! In any case, Chatterjee's duty has been changed—I'm in charge of the staff on this train. So stow your cleverness and fork out a second-class fare from Patna to Howrah, and the fine for ticketless travel as well."

'My pocket contained a grand total of five rupees—it wouldn't even pay for a third-class ticket, let alone second-class! I'd never seen stars in my eyes before, but I saw them now. And I began to sweat, even in the cold of that winter night.

"'Look Sahib—" I ventured.

"'Don't call me Sahib; my name is Mr Rhinoceros. And I'm as stubborn as one of the beasts. If you don't hand over your fare, I'll hand you over to the police at Howrah. Till then, I'll lock you into the carriage."

'What can I say, Pela— I'm Teniram of Potoldanga—I've seen plenty of sahibs in my time. If I had wanted to, I could have tossed the fellow out of the window of that moving train. But we're Vaishnavs, you see, it would have been wrong to take the life of a fellow creature. So, with great difficulty, I controlled my rage.'

Habul Sen said, 'Why do you eat goat if you've sworn not to take the lives of your fellow creatures?'

'Oh, goats are a different matter! They're dumb animals—the stomach of a Brahmin is their path to paradise. Eating goats amounts to being kind to the rest of creation, see? But what could I do with this sahib now? A nice fix I was in! God forbid that I should actually end up in jail! But God proved kind.

'The sahib had extracted a notebook from his pocket and was preparing to write something in it with his pencil, when suddenly there was a whirr of wings. The little bat had begun fluttering about again. Like me, he was travelling without a ticket. The sight of the checker must have alarmed him.

'It gave the sahib a mighty start. "What's that bird?" he demanded.

'I was about to tell him it was a little bat, but before I could speak, he broke out into yells. I don't know why that particular bat was so keen on noses—it clipped the sahib's with its wing as it flew past him.

'"What bird is that? How horrible it looks!" the sahib shrank back in fear. His whitewashed face was pallid.

'I realized this was my opportunity. "Haven't you ever seen this bird before?" I asked him.

'"No, never! It's only been six months since I left Africa for India. I've seen lions, rhinoceroses, but this—"

'The sahib was unable to finish his sentence. The little bat fluttered around the room again, almost digging its claws into the Englishman's face. It probably mistook it for a gourd.

'The sahib quavered, "Mister, does it bite?"

'"Oh yes," I assured him. "It's terribly poisonous. A single bite can kill a man in no more than than a minute."

'"What!" The sahib leapt into the air. Then he began pulling at my rugs: "Mister ... please ... for God's sake, let me have one of your blankets."

'"And leave me to die of its bites? Nothing doing!" I gripped them firmly.

"Heavens! What then?" So saying, the sahib did an extraordinary thing. He leapt for the chain and pulled it with all his might. Then he flung open the window and screamed at the top of his voice, "Help help!" The open window was all that the bat needed to fly over his shoulder and vanish into the darkness outside.

'The sahib stood dumbly for a while. Then he took a deep breath and remarked, "Thank goodness, the thing's gone. Nothing to be afraid of now, eh?"

'"No," I answered. "But you'd better be ready to fork out a fine of fifty rupees."

'The sahib's mouth fell open. "What on earth for?"

'"Pulling the chain without sufficient cause. The train's about to stop. And look here, Sahib, a little bat is a very harmless creature. Doesn't bite, doesn't do a thing to anyone. You work in the railways, yet you pulled the chain just because of a little bat. Never mind the fine, you're likely to lose your job for that!"

'Meanwhile the train was slowly drawing to a halt. Mr Rhinoceros stood blinking at me. In his alarm, he looked more like Mr Hare, a real rabbit.

'Then he seized my arm with both hands.

"'Look Mister, from this day you're my bosom friend. I'll escort you to a first-class saloon this minute—see how well you sleep. And when we get to Howrah, I'll treat you to a meal at Kelners. Just tell the guard, when he comes, that a thug armed with a pistol had broken into the carriage—that's why we pulled the chain. Agreed?"

'I had no choice. After all, how can one refuse such an earnest request?'

Tenida ended with a victorious laugh: 'Now off you go, Kyabla—get another four annas' worth of ghugni.'

Sage Dadhichi, Lord Viswakarma and Lots of Little Bugs

At the moment, I'm meditating in a deep forest. With admirable concentration, I might add. Only, there happen to be several insects flying about. They keep landing on my face, and I can't tell you how ghastly it feels. If one crawls up my nose and makes it tickle, another explores the mysteries of my inner ear. I've already made the mistake of gulping down a dozen. They didn't taste too bad—rather like fennel seeds, in fact—but what a ghastly stink! I felt like throwing up, but you can't throw up when you're meditating. Nor can I drive them away; I'm in a trance, you see. I have to stay absolutely still.

I had known from the beginning that it would all end badly. In fact, I had said as much to Habul—only our Indra, newly ascended to the divine state, was planning his visit to Lord Shiva's abode on Mount Kailash and wouldn't deign to listen. He said, 'Oh shut up! That's enough of your whining!

A forest's got to have insects, and they can't help landing on your face occasionally. Grin and bear it—how else can you become a great sage?'

True. But now I know why great sages have tempers as serene as the average hornet's nest and why the slightest provocation produces such a hail of curses. After all, there are limits to every man's patience. I'm sure even Shantanu, that gentle soul, would turn into Durbasa if he had to suffer the concentrated fury of those bugs.

This was turning out to be a real nuisance! Honestly speaking, I'm only Pelaram Banerjee, miserable, malarial, and dosed regularly with the juice of basak leaves. Why had I stepped into this snarl of sages and forests? I live in a house tucked away on a Potoldanga lane, on a forced diet of catfish curry and rice. A handful of *chanachur* I once popped into my mouth gave me such a stomach upset that I nearly popped it in earnest. And yet, meek as a cow myself, I had fallen into the clutches of Tenida—Tenida of the forty-two-inch chest, standing six feet tall.

You'll never know what that means unless you've actually run into Tenida. He's grown up thrashing every man alive, from the soldiers on the Maidan to rogue shopkeepers in the smuggled-goods market. If he raises his fist, you're afraid of a punch; if he bares his teeth, you're sure he'll bite. And it was in the thrall of this almighty being that I now sat in silent agony as a meditating sage.

What on earth could I do? I seemed to be sitting there forever. I could see that idiot Habul's nose sticking through a little hole in my forest glade. Almost maddened by insect bites, I was wondering if I should give it a quick punch when my disciple Dadhimukh made a sudden entrance.

Dadhimukh: O Master, hear my submission.

Myself: Speak, son, as I listen.

Dadhimukh: Yesternight, near dawn, I dreamed
A wondrous dream. O Sage, it seemed
I saw my Lord, in fair array
Through space, along the Milky Way
On a flaming chariot ride;
I watched, and in my awe I cried—
Yuck! Ugh! Pthoo!

What else but those infernal insects! Choking and spluttering, Dadhimukh spat the lot he had swallowed all over me—the cheek of my callow disciple! I boiled with rage from head to toe. My pigtail stood erect in sacred fury. But cursing him would ruin everything. I contented myself with thinking, 'Wait, my son, I'll deal with you by and by.'

Smiling, I said:

Tis true, a mystery does in this appear
Thy feeble wit
Can't fathom it.
Come close; I'll whisper it in thy young ear.

Dadhimukh stared at me open-mouthed. The lines he had hoped to hear had vanished—he didn't know what to do. He looked around helplessly.

I began again:

Why standst thou there?
Come close, and near my lips place thou thy ear.
The wondrous words I cannot else tell thee
Come close, dear boy; my son, come close to me.

Dadhimukh's young and foolish. Hesitantly, he laid his ear close to my lips and I replied immediately. Opening my mouth wide, I trapped a whole swarm of bugs. Then I spat them neatly and noisily back over Dadhimukh's cheeks, nose, mouth and forehead. A loving guru's blessing!

Dadhimukh shrieked. The drop scene was abruptly lowered. Hitting me on the nose, the bamboo pole descended sharply. Leaving the scene incomplete, the second act came to an untimely end.

Habul, dressed as Indra, and Tenida, dressed as Viswakarma, rushed on to the stage. 'What was all that about?' thundered Tenida. 'Pela, what d'you mean by upsetting everything?'

'What do *you* mean?' I countered defiantly.

Tenida gnashed his teeth. 'D'you want to ruin the play, you scamp? What made you spit into Kyabla's face like that? You've made a proper mess of the scene ... just listen to the audience laughing!'

'Kyabla spat at me first,' I retorted.

'Hmmm,' said Tenida. 'I should knock your two heads together like a pair of young coconuts. Well, what's done is done. Now you'll have to manage the next few scenes properly, understand? Any more funny business and I'll punch your nose into a nosegay.'

'You can say what you like,' said I. 'But who's going to sit on stage eating those bugs, tell me?'

'You will,' roared Tenida. 'By God you will. What's theatre without swallowing a few bugs? One has to eat flies, mosquitoes –'

'Rats, bats . . .' Habul joined in.

'And mats, too,' finished Tenida. 'In fact, it wouldn't be extraordinary if you ate a mattress. Or a bedstead. That's what's called theatre, see?'

'What, do you have to eat all that to act?' I protested feebly.

'Oh yes you do. What d'you know of these things? Never heard of Danibabu, have you? When he played the role of Sita, he swallowed a monument before every performance.'

'A monument!'

'Yes, yes, a monument! Now get lost, and not another squawk out of you! The curtain's just going up—scoot—go revise your lines!'

Scowling like a scarecrow in an eggplant patch, I went and sat on one side of the stage. Monuments indeed! No other place for tall tales—who in all mankind eats monuments? But protest and be slapped for it. All I could do was swallow Tenida's giant fib in silence.

Grace the stage and eat bugs. Why, my dear chaps, I suppose my catfish curry would have stuck in my throat if I hadn't got myself involved in your play. I, Pelaram Banerjee, of weak stomach and sickly spleen, why did I have to play Sage Dadhichi with a face full of prickly beard? I had fallen among villains, and was doomed to suffer.

There I'd been, sitting comfortably on the Chatterjees' front step, watching an enthusiastic rehearsal. But no one could be found to play the role of Dadhichi. Tenida, casting his saucer-like eyes about, suddenly pounced on me and seized my shoulder: 'Ah, got him!'

'Oi, oi!' I protested.

'No oi-oi's from you,' growled Tenida. 'Say "aye aye" instead. You look like an ascetic anyway—harmless and goat-like. We'll stick a nice goat's beard on your face—you'll see how it suits you! You'll look exactly like that old gaffer at the Rays'.'

And this was the result.

I didn't appear in the third act. Sitting in gloomy silence by the stage, I took off the false beard and swatted mosquitoes for dear life. No, this was insufferable. Come my cue, and I'd have to meditate again. Meditate, and I'd be attacked by more bugs. Most deadly bugs, too.

What could I do?

Every fibre of my body was quivering with rage. Out of the kindness of my heart, I was playing a role in their wretched play. That seemed more than enough. But to insult me into the bargain, bullying me like that and threatening to punch my nose into a nosegay! Tenida was really getting above himself. What if his nose was as lofty as a pyramid and mine as flat as a Chinaman's? To insult my nose for all that! Well, hold it. Not so fast. I'd bring him to a sticky end yet, and watch him squirm with this snub nose of mine held as high as the mythical mountain of Mainak.

But, in plain fact, what could I do?

I thought and thought, but to no avail. Meanwhile Tenida was on the stage, delivering a magnificent speech and leaping around so wildly that the Chatterjees' ancient, bug-infested mattress began to groan ominously. It was difficult to tell whether he was acting in a play or doing the high jump.

Stage manager Habul came hurrying past. 'Here, Pela, why're you sitting in the dark like a ghost?'

'Brother Habul, give me some tea,' I begged. 'My throat feels as parched as a dry log.'

Habul turned up his nose. 'Oh shut up! Don't drink so much tea . . . the way you played your role, you shouldn't need it!'

Adding insult to injury, was he? I bared my teeth and made a horrible face at Habul, but it was lost in the darkness.

Should I do the disappearing act, beard and all? Dash straight home while the going was good? It'd serve them right if they looked for Dadhichi before his next scene, and found the holy man missing. But no, that wasn't a good idea. Tomorrow morning would be sure to bring retribution . . . who'd save me then? Potoldanga's celebrated Tenida would send me straight to heaven with a couple of his celebrated slaps.

No, no, none of all this. I'd kill the snake without breaking the stick. I'd make them bleed, but they'd have to swallow the thrust with the smiles still on their faces. I'd add a wisdom tooth to Tenida's thirty-two shiners. And I wouldn't spare his henchman Habul either, that obsequious insect of a stage manager.

'Lord, give me light,' I prayed silently. 'A light in the darkness.'

And the light appeared.

I said to Habul, 'Brother Habul, I'm going home for five minutes.'

'Why?' asked Habul in alarm.

'This stomach of mine—it's feeling a little . . .'

'That does it,' said Habul. 'You chronic invalids and your weak stomachs. It looks as if you'll let us down in the end. You're to go on in a little while, remember?'

'Don't worry, I'll be back in five minutes,' I assured him.

To myself, I said, 'We'll see how strong your stomachs are by and by. Want to feed me monuments before I act? We'll see if you can swallow something stronger!'

Within the promised five minutes, I was back. My uncle was a doctor, and it hadn't taken me long to ransack his medicine cupboard. I had found the magic drug. Nearly an hour remained before my entrance—plenty of time for me to do my little job.

The big tea kettle was simmering on the stove. I approached it quietly. No one noticed; they were all peering out of the wings, absorbed in the play. Tenida was leaping about like an energetic Bheem. What claps he was getting! Wait a bit—I'd see how much applause he wanted in a while.

His pyramid of a nose held high in triumph, Tenida returned to the wings. 'How did I do, Habul?' he asked, grinning broadly.

'Oh, you were brilliant!' replied Habul humbly. 'Who but you could play a part like that? The audience is shouting "Bravo, bravo!"'

I knew why the audience was cheering. The poor fools had no idea whether Tenida had been playing Bheem or Viswakarma. But the really interesting scene was yet to be staged.

Tenida shook the stage with his yell of 'Tea! Someone bring in the tea!'

Habul fled.

The drop curtain rose once again. I sat rapt in meditation as Sage Dadhichi and manfully ate bugs. My disciple Dadhimukh was standing at a prudent distance—experience had made him wise.

Enter Viswakarma and Indra. Also known as Tenida and Habul.

Habul began:

Great sage, our holy master.
I come to you at Lord Shiva's command.
The lightning bolt that from your ancient bones
Is to be drawn—

Tenida continued:

Shall by the best of Viswakarma's art
Into a mighty weapon be transformed
The planets nine, and all their several seas
Shall tremble with its roar and everything
Still or moving, quick or dead, shall burn
In its bright flame –

Then he added a little soliloquy: 'Ooh, what a stomach ache I'm getting!'

'My stomach's churning too,' added Habul in a hollow whisper.

I just glanced at them out of the corner of my eye. They had sworn they could digest monuments. I'd see what their digestions were really worth!

'Peace, peace,' I rebuked.

First let me muse upon the sacred name.
Until my trance is broken
Let not a word be spoken,
I will surrender then my ancient frame.

So saying, I sank into meditation. My trance wasn't to be

broken in a hurry. The bugs persisted in their attack, but never mind. As I sowed, so should Tenida and Habul reap. Hot tea and a strong purgative combined—could I afford to let them off so quickly now?

Tenida's facial contortions were impossible to ignore. 'Get on with that meditation, Pela, quick! The cramps I'm getting in my stomach!'

'Quiet!' I said sternly.

Disturb my rapt devotion,
And I'll curse you as the only proper caution—

Do you think I was really meditating? Poppycock! Out of the corner of my eye, I was watching Tenida's face grow ashen. Habul didn't look much better. God was kind indeed.

'Oh Pela, I'm done for!' moaned Tenida abjectly. 'Come out of that trance, quick, I beg of you—I'm falling at your feet, Pela!'

Habul joined in. 'Brother Pela, I'm dying too!'

I sat deaf and unmoving. Do what you will! The trance of a sage—one about to become a martyr, too! Was it to be broken so easily?

'Good God, I'm finished!' Tenida disappeared in a flying leap, in the direction of the dark mango orchards. Habul followed at his heels.

And the play?

Need I say any more about it?

A Fishy Tale

Go to Bengal and you'll find
You can't leave your fate behind.

Well, the question of going to Bengal didn't arise in my case—I happen to be there already, a true son of the soil. Actually, I was paying a visit to Bangeshwari Mistanna Bhandar, the local sweet shop.

I had just risen from the sickbed, malaria having laid me low for a week. My appetite's keen at the best of times, and that recent bout of illness had left me craving food from the depths of my soul. I was hungry day and night—I could have swallowed the heavens, devoured the pits of hell. My thirty-two nerves writhed in my famished stomach like a bed of cobras. And, in addition to that eager belly, I possessed an eccentric spleen—the Himalayas swallowed whole wouldn't appease its hunger.

Therefore, I was sitting in Bangeshwari Mistanna

Bhandar, about to polish off three large pieces of rajbhog in my best style. But go to Bengal and you'll find—

A lion's roar rang through my ear: 'There you are, Pela—living off the fat of the land, eh?'

My spleen sprang up, did a quick dance, and collapsed abruptly. I'd set a hearty bite into that rajbhog—now, like Trishanku, whom the gods had suspended between heaven and earth, the sweet remained poised between my jaw and my hand. Only a dribble of syrup ran down and settled on my handloom kurta.

I looked around. Who could it be but that universal terror—Tenida of Potoldanga? Tenida, five hands tall, with the build of an all-in wrestler and the distinction of having beaten the hide off every thug on the streets, not to mention the occasional football referee when Mohonbagan lost a match. The syrup-soaked rajbhog in my mouth suddenly tasted as bitter as quinine.

'Weren't you down with fever just the other day?' demanded Tenida. 'Already eating this rubbish? This time you'll kill yourself for sure.'

'Kill myself?' I mumbled fearfully.

'Absolutely. Not a doubt of it.' Tenida sat down noisily in the chair next to me. 'But I might make one last attempt to save you.'

So saying, Tenida performed the charitable act of saving my life by popping the remaining two pieces of rajbhog into his mouth and consuming them with relish. Then, with another lusty roar, he called, 'Four more rajbhog here!'

My own feast had been doomed from the start, but it wasn't before he had lightened my pocket by three and a half rupees that Tenida considered my life out of danger. Weeping inwardly, I left the shop. But, just as I was planning to sneak past the corner of Hedua and make a dash for Duff Street, Tenida's hand closed firmly on my shoulder. It wasn't so much a grip as arrest by main force. I felt as if a half-tonne sack had suddenly dropped on my shoulder. My whole frame shrank in agony.

'Oi Pela, why're you running away?'

I turned wooden with terror from crown to toe. 'N-n-n-n-no, no—w-w-why would I r-r-run away . . .'

'In that case, my cherub, why were you scuttling off like a sneaky little squirrel? Don't try to be too clever, Pela. You're coming with me.'

'Where to?'

'Dumdum.'

'Why Dumdum?' I asked in astonishment.

Tenida lost his temper. 'You're a donkey!'

'What for?' I asked.

'For carrying the dhobi's bundle,' growled Tenida. 'For eating grass fresh grown on the municipal waste dump. For braying "eee-yore" at intervals. It's Sunday and we're going to Dumdum for some fishing. Don't you understand that, you nincompoop?'

'If you're going fishing, go ahead. Why drag me in?'

'Who's going to bait my hook for me if you don't come along? I tell you straight, I'm not messing about with any worms.'

'Wonderful,' I said. 'You'll catch the fish and leave the worms to me.'

'Shut up—you needn't stand whining in the street. Now quick march, we're going to Sealdah. There's a train to Dumdum in fifteen minutes.'

I stood hesitating, only to have Tenida yank me off my feet. His tug almost tore my arm from my shoulder. 'Ooh, I'm a goner!' I yelled in agony.

'Gone where? You're going to Dumdum with me, I'm not letting you go anywhere else. Come on. Ready—one, two . . .'

But before he could say three, I seemed to sprout wings and go soaring through the air. My head spun, my ears buzzed. When I came to, I found Tenida had me incarcerated in the second-class compartment of a tram.

In a voice like distant thunder, he assured me, 'If I catch any fish, I'll spare you a little from the tail.'

The villain! As if I had never learnt to eat a decent piece of fish! But I didn't have the courage to argue. Cop it from Tenida—and you were sure to pop it shortly. So I kept my mouth shut. We proceeded to Sealdah in silence, and got off the train at the English bazaar in Dumdum.

We walked a little further along the railway line in the direction of Bon-ga and came to an ancient bungalow surrounded by orchards. 'Come on,' said Tenida, 'we can fish here.'

I retreated three paces. 'Are you out of your mind?' I gasped. 'Who's going to fish in there? I'm sure the place is haunted!'

Tenida bared his teeth at me like an ape. 'Haunted my foot! This is our own family farmhouse—how on earth would ghosts come here? And if I catch one trespassing, I'll knock out all its thirty-two teeth with a single punch! Come along, come along—'

Calling silently upon the gods, I followed Tenida.

Overgrown and derelict as it looked on the outside, the house wasn't bad once we were in it. There was an enormous flower garden. Though few flowers remained, some statues were scattered about. There were some fruit trees, too—mango, *litchi*, coconut and the like. In the middle stood a small, old-fashioned building. The whitewash was flaking off the walls, the bricks coming loose, but the place had charm. Cane chairs were arranged on the huge verandah.

Stepping onto the porch, Tenida gave a mighty yell: 'Hey, Jaga . . .'

From distant regions came the reply: 'I'm a-coming—'

An Oriya caretaker hurried up to us. 'Dadababu, you've a-come?'

'I've a-come,' agreed Tenida. 'Where were you all this while, you wretch? Now hurry up and get us a few nice tender coconuts.'

'I'll be a-getting them—'

So saying, Jaga swarmed up the nearest coconut tree like a monkey. Within a few minutes he had brought down the coconuts. Draining four in quick succession, Tenida queried, 'Everything ready, Jaga?'

'Aye.'

'Hooks, floats, bait . . . everything?'

'Aye,' confirmed Jaga.

'Come on, Pela—let's make for the pond.'

We were soon at the steps leading down to the water. Splendid steps they were too—paved in white stone. Except for a slight film of moss, the water was quite clear. Palm fronds, rustling in the breeze, cast their shade over the bank. You could hear birds calling. No spot could be more perfect for fishing. Two colossal rods and tackles lay on the steps—looking at them, you'd think we were planning to bag a shark, if not a crocodile.

'Got the bait, Jaga?' asked Tenida.

'Aye.'

'Dug us some worms?'

'Aye.'

'Then off you go. You can cook us some *khichdi*. Come on, Pela, get to work. Here, thread a worm on the end of this hook.'

I assumed my most piteous expression. 'A worm?'

Tenida unleashed a furious bellow: 'What else? Have I brought you here to stare at your silly face? Who wants to see something that looks like a drooping banana? Don't

161

make me lose my temper, Pela, the blood's rising to my head. Here, take the worms.'

Had I left home at an unlucky moment today? All I could hope for now was to return to Potoldanga alive, and with my dignity intact. Perhaps the sight of my woebegone face stirred Tenida's compassion. He said, 'There, there, don't fret! All right, if I catch any fish, the heads are mine, the rest all yours. A gentleman's word is his bond. Now come on, bait those hooks.'

I knew quite well what Tenida's catch would be like. A close acquaintance with worms was all I was likely to get out of it. What could you call this but fate?

But a gentleman's word is his bond. And Tenida was soon to learn how terrible that bond could be.

We cast our lines and sat waiting.

We seemed to be waiting forever. Our eyes ached with staring at the water. But to what end? The floats hovered motionless on the surface, as erect as monuments on an empty field. Not a bob, not a stir—nothing!

'Tenida, where are the fish?' I said after a while.

'Shut up, don't talk,' admonished Tenida. 'You'll scare them away.'

Another half hour passed. The float stood erect, cheeky as a cocked thumb. The gently rippling water made it sway a little, but that was all.

I asked again, 'O Tenida, what's up with the fish?'

'Oh be quiet!' scolded Tenida in exasperation. 'Why d'you talk so much? These carp weigh anything between ten and twenty seers—d'you expect to nab them so easily? It's a major business. Now keep your mouth screwed shut.'

Silence again. After a while, I was just about to say something, when the sight of Tenida's face brought me to an abrupt stop. He was almost falling over his rod in excitement. His eyeballs were popping from their sockets.

Sure enough—we seemed to be seeing the impossible. Were our eyes playing tricks on us? The float was literally dancing with bites.

Our goggling eyes were almost eating up that bobbing float now. Tenida's two hands clutched the rod grimly— one jerk and we'd have our catch. My heart pounded to the rhythm of the dancing cork. In low, hoarse tones, I cried, 'Tenida!'

'Praise to the holy Fish Goddess!' With a mighty heave-ho, Tenida yanked the line out of the water. Making an unearthly noise, the hook flew through the air. A shower of torn palm leaves fell from above. But the hook? Quite bare—never mind fish, there wasn't even a fish scale on it!

'Ah, the blighter's given us the slip!' exclaimed Tenida. 'All right, all right. Let's see where he goes. It's my day or his! Here Pela, stick another worm on that hook—'

The force of Tenida's tug had told me what sort of fish he'd land. It wouldn't be a fish at all—it would be nothing less than a hippopotamus. But there was no point in saying so—I'd just be cuffed. It was my fate to hook worms, and I went on hooking them.

But the carp seemed to be wriggling around Tenida's bait in dozens! Scarcely had a couple of minutes passed when, lo and behold, float number two began to bob.

'Tenida, careful now,' I warned.

'Do you think I'll let him slip through my hands again? A sly one, is he? But don't talk, Pela—quiet! One, two—and three!'

The hook whizzed through the air again. More palm leaves fell. But the fish? Alas, there were none.

'Escaped again?' exclaimed Tenida. 'The luck of the rascal! But I'll settle him. Stick on another worm, Pela! Today, it's him or me.'

This was turning out to be a most extraordinary affair. No sooner was the line cast than the float began to dip—reel it in, and the hook came up bare. What could it mean? Such things didn't usually happen, nor were they meant to!

Tenida was left scratching his head. After we had reeled in the line about eight times in succession, the palm tree overhead began to look quite bald, but of fish we saw not a fin or scale.

'What's this?' wondered Tenida. 'Are there ghosts about?'

We hadn't even noticed Jaga standing behind us. With a sudden grin that showed a mouthful of *paan*-reddened teeth, he answered, 'If you please, it isn't ghosts, it's them crabbers.'

'Crabbers? You mean crabs?'

'Aye,' agreed Jaga.

'Then I'll finish off the grandfather of all crabs!' Tenida's roar shook the heavens. 'Were the rascals growing fat on my bait all this while? That's the end of their feast! Now fetch me a big dish, Jaga, or a basket.'

'Dish? Basket?' I asked in amazement. 'What use will that be?'

'You shut up, Pela—ask me one more question and I'll rattle your brains with a slap. Off you go, Jaga—run! Fetch me that basket!'

I wondered fearfully if Tenida had lost it at last. Was he proposing to pursue the fish through the pond with a basket in his hand? But no . . .

What followed was a sight to be seen, a marvel worthy of the sorceress Bhanumati. This time, when the float bobbed, Tenida didn't heave it ashore. Instead, he reeled in the line very carefully. As the float approached the bank, an enormous red crab came into view, clinging tightly to the hook. 'The blighter will let go the moment the hook comes to the surface,' said Tenida. 'So, just before I raise my rod, be sure to hold the basket ready under the water, Jaga. We'll see who's smarter, me or those confounded crabs!'

Thus began a most thrilling hunt. This time, the crabs had to concede to Tenida's superior cunning. Within half an hour, the basket was piled high.

Two enormous rods had reeled in a catch of a good forty crabs.

'Not bad,' declared Tenida. 'Nothing wrong with crab curry. How's the khichdi getting on, Jaga?'

But a gentleman's word is his bond. I never forget a promise.

I reminded him, 'Tenida, the heads are yours, the rest mine, remember?'

'Hey, no—' began Tenida in alarm.

'Oh yes,' said I.

Tenida's look of triumph changed to one of despair. 'So then?'

'So then, the heads, meaning the claws, are yours. The rest is my share.'

'What d'you mean?' Tenida uttered a hollow cry.

'A gentleman's word is his bond,' I pointed out.

'But don't crabs have any heads, then?'

They have ends, if not heads, but I didn't tell him that. 'The only heads they have are those claws,' I said firmly.

Tenida stood speechless for a while, then sat down slowly. 'Pela, was this what you had in mind all along? O-ho-ho—'

Let him scold as he liked. The sorrow of parting with three and a half rupees at Bangeshwari Mistanna Bhandar was still fresh in my memory.

For two days now, I've been eating crab curry with great relish. But I can't tell you if Tenida has been enjoying the claws as much. For when I met him in the street the other day, he hunched his shoulders and hurried past, pretending not to recognize me.

Tenida and the Yeti

'Yetis indeed! All bogus!' declared Kyabla.

Habul Sen protested loudly: 'Oh yes—it's bogus because you say so! A monastry in the Himalayas has actually preserved the skin of a yeti—what about that?'

'That could be the skin of any large monkey,' said Kyabla sagely, lifting his bespectacled nose higher into the air.

'Well, lots of Englishmen have written about yetis,' retorted Habul.

'But nobody's actually seen one. It's exactly the same with ghost stories—everyone tells them, but can you find me a single person who's seen a ghost with his own eyes?'

I was about to comment, when Tenida joined our group on the ledge that ran around the Chatterjees' house. He looked at us sternly and demanded in gravelly tones, 'What were you three arguing about?'

'Yetis,' I replied.

'Oh, yetis.' Tenida sat down impressively. 'What do you kids know about such things? You'd better ask me.'

'Oh look, it's Grandpa,' commented Habul.

'Shut up,' ordered Tenida. 'If you're going to be disrespectful to your elders and betters, I'll give your ears—'

I filled in the gap: 'A year's worth of twisting.'

'Yes, yes, correct!' Tenida thumped my back till the vertebrae shifted. Then he continued, 'Yeti? You mean—what d'you call it—the Ab—Ab—Abo—'

'Abominable Snowman,' supplied Kyabla.

'To hell with it—it sounds disgusting in English. Yeti's much better. You think it doesn't exist? I've seen one with my own two eyes.'

'You?' I squawked in amazement.

'Surprised, are you?' Tenida glowered at me. 'Who'd see a yeti, if not me? You? Some cheek you've got, considering you were nursing yourself on catfish curry till the other day—'

Habul intervened. 'No, why on earth should Pela have seen a yeti? It's Premen Mitra's Ghanada who usually sees such things—when did you take over?'

Ghanada's very name made Tenida put his hands to his head. 'Ghanada? Why, he's a hero! Never mind your yeti, he's probably had tea with its grandfather! But why should that mean I haven't seen one?'

'No such thing,' said Kyabla. 'Nothing's beyond your powers. But when and how did you see it?'

'Want to hear all that?' replied Tenida. 'Then nip down to the nearest snack vendor and fetch six annas' worth of *jhalmuri*—quick!' Giving my back a terrific thump, he elaborated. 'Very quick.'

The thump made my blood boil. 'I don't have any money,' I said.

'In that case, Kyabla, you'd better fork out—quick!'

Kyabla obeyed, for fear of a similar blow. And he wasn't just quick, he was very quick.

Munching on his muri, Tenida began. 'Guess where I spent a month of my summer vacation this year.'

'At Gobordanga,' I said. 'You had gone there to eat mangoes at your aunt's.'

'Oh, I just said that to dupe you all. I had actually gone on a Himalayan expedition.'

'What? Really?' gasped Habul.

'Have you ever known me to tell lies?' roared Tenida.

'God forbid!' said Kyabla piously. 'Lies from you? But where were you bound for? The summit of Everest?'

'Not on your life—everyone goes to the top of Everest; it's far too easy. It won't be long before schoolchildren are picnicking on the summit. I had gone in search of a higher peak.'

'Is there one?' We were all startled.

'You never know—some faces of the Himalayas are always dark with mists and clouds—no one's ever explored the mysteries of those secret heights. Why, during the last war, two American pilots declared they had glimpsed a mountain peak at a height of thirty-five thousand feet. But then it vanished from sight, no one knows where.'

'Did you find that peak, Tenida?' I wanted to know.

'Shut up, idiot! If I had, wouldn't you have seen my picture in all the newspapers? Would I still be sitting in the classrooms of your City College and answering for absentees? They'd have carried me off to Delhi in triumph by now—I'd have received one of those—what d'you call them—state horrors.'

'State honours,' corrected Kyabla.

'Same thing.' Tenida emptied his paper bag of jhalmuri and ordered, 'Now be quiet—don't disturb my concentration. No, I didn't find that new peak. It was one of those—er—those storms of snow and ice—'

'A blizzard,' supplied Kyabla.

'Yes, well, such a blizzard blew up that all the Sherpas fled. What could I do but return disappointed to Kalimpong? Uncle Kutti's brother-in-law is a doctor there, and he put me up at his house.'

'Where did you see the yeti, then?' I asked. 'In the blizzard?'

'No, in Kalimpong.'

'A yeti in Kalimpong?' screeched Habul. 'Find some other place for your tales! Haven't I been to Kalimpong? A yeti there? Why, we'll be expecting one in Potoldanga next!'

'We might indeed,' said Tenida gravely. 'It's perfectly possible.'

'What?' we gasped in chorus.

'That's right,' declared Tenida. 'They're invisible, which means that you can't see them most of the time. That's why people see their footprints, but can't catch sight of them. They can go wherever they want whenever they want to. Besides, they can resume their visible forms at will, which is a sight one had better not see. I saw it in Kalimpong, and don't ever want to see it again.'

'But how did a yeti get there in the first place?' I asked.

'Who knows where a yeti is and isn't? Perhaps this very minute, as we talk, there's an invisible yeti standing behind us and laughing its head off.'

All three of us looked warily over our shoulders.

'No, you won't see it unless it chooses to show itself to you. Do you think, you fools, that it's so easy to see a yeti?' scolded Tenida. 'You need special luck for that.'

'And I suppose you were specially lucky?' asked Kyabla.

Tenida thumped his knee. 'I was indeed.'

'And you saw the yeti right in Kalimpong?' asked Habul.

'Of course.'

'I suppose the yeti was drinking tea in a restaurant?' suggested Kyabla. 'Or had it gone for a stroll on the far bank of the Chitrabhanu river?'

'Being funny, are you?' Tenida let out a roar. 'Joking about yetis?'

'Let him be,' interceded Habul. 'He's just a little milksop.'

'Milksop, is he? He needs to be drunk up like milk then. If I hear you gibber like a gerbil just one more time, Kyabla, I'll punch that bespectacled nose of yours till—'

'Till it "knows" better,' I supplied.

'Right you are.' Tenida's hand, about to thump my back

again, swung through empty air—I had already skipped out of reach.

With an aggrieved expression, he said, 'Damn, not a back at hand when you need one! Rubbish!'

'But the yeti?' reminded Habul.

'Hang on, you oaf, let me get into the mood.' Tenida screwed up his mouth like carrot crumble and noisily scratched the tip of his nose. Then he continued, 'Yes, it was all to do with being funny about yetis. In fact, I began by treating the whole thing as a joke. But I soon realized the truth. You can act clever in most places, but none of your tricks with a yeti.'

'Your tricks didn't work with him, then?' I asked.

'No.' Tenida paused like someone deep in thought. Then he said, 'You see, on my return from that expedition, I had gone down to Kalimpong, where I was enjoying a well-earned rest. Dr Harekeshto's got a flourishing poultry—his hens cackled like alarm clocks in the morning and were served up as curries and cutlets for lunch and dinner. It was all very comfortable, and one day I made the acquaintance of a French tourist. You know how well I speak French.'

'You do?' exclaimed Kyabla.

'Don't I just! De-la-grande-Mephistopheles—yak-yak—what language was that, then?'

'Fluent French,' said Habul gravely. 'Go on.'

'Well, I soon rose high in the man's regard. You know what it is with these tourists, don't you? They're endlessly curious about everything. "Why do Indians wear pigtails? Why are your crows so black? Your gods must be very fierce if you keep yelling 'Horrible! Horrible!' to appease them (he meant *Hari Bol*). Can Indian beetles sing like birds? Are the moles in this country descended from pigs?" It was in the course of asking all these questions that one day he asked, "Now then, Monsieur, you've been to the Himalayas—did you ever happen to see a yeti?"

'I couldn't resist pulling the man's leg. His name was Lelefan. So I began in style, "What do you think, M. Lelefan? You ask me if I've seen a yeti? Why, I caught one and brought it back with me!"

"'What? Brought a yeti back with you?' Lelefan gulped thrice. "But no one's ever managed to capture one yet!"

'I gave him a couple of taps on the chest and declared, "This is Teniram of Potoldanga—I can do what others can't. Why, I've got a yeti at home!"

'Lelefan gaped at me awhile. Then he screwed up his face as if he was going to burst into tears, gulped thrice like someone swallowing live mosquitoes and finally managed to gasp, "Will you show me your yeti?"

"'Why not?" I said.

'Hearing my reply, Lelefan began to bounce up and down so excitedly that he tripped over a stone and fell flat on his back. If I hadn't seized him by the legs and pulled him up, he'd have rolled straight into a pit thirty feet below. Then he grabbed both my hands and danced around for three full minutes, yelling "tango, tango".

'"Let's go and see your yeti right now," he proposed.

'"That won't do, Monsieur," I replied. "I can't put him on show at will. He sleeps for three and a half days of the week and is awake for the other three and a half. If you disturb him when he's asleep, one swipe of his arm will—"'

'Send you to Armenia,' I supplied.

'Right,' said Tenida. 'So I told Lelefan, "The yeti's been asleep since yesterday. He'll wake up shortly after noon the day after tomorrow. In the evening, once he's had a meal, and perked up, I'll take you to see him."

'"I can take pictures of him with my camera, can't I?" asked Lelefan.

'"Good heavens, don't do any such thing! Yetis don't like cameras at all—he might bite you. Then you'll perish of hydrophobia."

'"Can you get hydrophobia from a yeti's bite?"'

'"Hydrophobia's nothing. You could burn up with black fever, or be massacred by malaria, or crippled by cholera, or plagued by pernicious alopecia or even suffer a Sibilant Sanskrit Ending."'

Kyabla tried to object. 'How could you suffer a Sibilant Sanskrit—'

'You shut up, Kyabla, stop nagging like a nit. Hearing my words, Lelefan exclaimed in French, "Mi Ghott!" That means "My God!"'

'Do you say "Mi Ghott?" in French, then?' asked Kyabla sceptically.

'Shut up, I say!' yelled Tenida. 'If you argue with me one

more time, I'll have you fetch a rupee's worth of potato chops. You can call it a fine.'

Kyabla shrank, exclaiming, 'Mi Ghott! There, I won't argue any more, go on.'

'But you'll still be fined eight annas' worth of potato chops. So scoot—quick!'

'Yes,' I added. 'Very quick.'

Wearing a scowl that made his face look blacker than a piece of fried eggplant, Kyabla fetched the chops.

'Fries them well, that chap.' Tenida dug his teeth into a chop. 'Mephistopheles, as you might say.'

'But the yeti?' I pleaded.

'Yes, yes—the yeti. You see, by then, I had hit on a plan. Reaching home, I shared it with Harekeshto babu. He's Uncle Kutti's brother-in-law, and loves a good prank. He agreed. All I had to do after that was rope Kaila in.'

'Who's Kaila?' asked Habul.

'Oh, a Nepali lad about our age, the assistant at Harekeshto Babu's clinic. He's always looking for mischief. "Daju ramro—ramro," he said when he heard my plan. That means, "Dada, brilliant, quite brilliant!"'

'Meanwhile, time was hanging heavy on the sahib's hands.

'"Is your yeti still asleep?"

'"Snoring."

'"He will wake up on time, won't he?"'

'"On time? He'll sit up on the stroke of noon, not a second later!"

'Well, the great day arrived. In Harekeshto Babu's large

hall upstairs, I rigged up a black curtain. We'd planned to have only a dim light in the room. Slowly, I would draw back the curtain to reveal the yeti. A minute or two, and I'd drop the curtain on him again.'

'But the yeti—' I began.

'Shut up, you dish of catfish curry! What yeti? Harekeshto Babu's house boasted a magnificent bearskin. Our plan was to drape Kaila in it, put a hideous Nepali mask on his face, and let him leap around a little, yelling some gibberish—Drum drum! Yahoo, yahoo! Monsieur Lelefan's teeth would start chattering with terror.

'With this end in mind, we got everything ready. When the sahib arrived, a lamp was flickering faintly in the room and a black curtain hung before him. All of the previous day, I'd regaled him with grisly tales of yetis. As he stepped into the room, I could tell his heart was pounding.

'Harekeshto Babu had come to watch the fun; so had his compounder Golak Babu. We had managed to create quite an atmosphere. With a "One—two—three!" I drew back the curtain. And—'

'And?' we demanded in a chorus.

'Good heavens! It was no Kaila that stood before us! His bearskin had fallen off, his mask had been knocked off his face—he sprawled senseless on the floor like a flattened frog. A giant figure loomed before us, stretching up to the ceiling. I can't describe what it looked like— neither man nor gorilla, bristling with spiky pale fur, eyes blazing like twin cauldrons . . . In a voice like the roar of three lions at once, it said in clear Bengali, "Want to see a yeti, do you? Then why a poor copy—here's the real article!"

'So saying, it laughed thunderously. Thirty knife-sharp teeth flashed in the darkness. Then suddenly, before our very eyes, that awful form seemed to melt away, dissolving into a cloud of pale smoke that vanished as suddenly as it had appeared. The icy blast of a Himalayan blizzard swept over us, freezing our very blood; the closed doors were wrenched off their hinges and hit the ground some ten feet away. Then, lashing through the forests of pine and sal, that wild wind sped shrieking towards Nathula.

'I stood there petrified. The sahib was gibbering on the floor. The compounder was out cold. Harekeshto Babu lay swooning in his chair, mumbling deliriously, "Coramine! Coramine! Give it to me, not the sahib, I'm going to have a heart attack any minute . . ."'

Tenida paused. 'You see, that's what a real yeti's like. Don't get too smart with him—you won't live long if you do. And don't you ask to see him, either—you're better off without it.'

We sat dumbfounded for a while. Then Kyabla said airily, 'Poppycock.'

'Poppycock?' Tenida glared at him. 'Those yetis are omniscient. Talking too much as usual, aren't you? Can you be sure that the lion-like paw of an invisible yeti isn't stealing over your shoulder this very—'

Calling upon his ancestors to save him, Kyabla leapt off the step and fled for home.

Translator's Note

Translating stories that one has grown up with is both pleasurable and frustrating. When I read Narayan Gangopadhyay's Tenida tales in my childhood, it was for the fun of getting to know the four heroes of Potoldanga—quick-witted Kyabla, Dhaka-born Habul Sen, nervous Pela and, of course, Tenida himself, with his big nose and even bigger appetite. I also read the stories for the sense of carnival that they brought to everyday life—for the tall tales swapped at every adda, the incredible characters encountered on vacations, and the zest with which rasagollas, mutton ghugni and even catfish curry were enjoyed. Returning to the books later, I found even more pleasure in the sketches of the city and the times that surround the central figures of Tenida, Pela, Habul and Kyabla. While the longer tales, such as *Charmurti*, take the four Potoldanga boys out of Kolkata, most of the short stories are set in the city. They conjure up pictures of an unhurried past, of large joint families, good food and endless leisure for conversation. As student life takes me further and further away from Kolkata, this is a portrait of the city's past that I especially cherish.

But the things that make reading Narayan Gangopadhyay's stories fun also make translating them a challenge. For all the simplicity of the tales, the world of Tenida is a richly material and social one, full of things and places, people and events. References to an urban geography now radically changed, or to foods forgotten except in the deep recesses of north Kolkata complicate the translator's task. So do the materials of language, the punning insults ('kaan tene Kanpur-e patthiye debo'), polyglot phrases ('De la grande Mephistopheles') and other pieces of verbal craft that go into the making of seemingly careless comedy. Many of these expressions do not transfer easily into English. Some jokes have been lost, some phrases translated only approximately. Hopefully, this will not lessen the fun of knowing Tenida and his friends. Their essential spirit is hard to quench—in any language, time, or place.

Moreover, language, time and place are not really what they seem in Gangopadhyay's fiction. I was well into the translation, vexed by the unavailability of modern-day equivalents for what I thought was the vanished world of the author's own youth, when I realized that such a world had probably never existed. At least not in the upheavals of 1940s, when the first stories were written, nor for the young Gangopadhyay himself, an active freedom fighter and member of the radical Anushilan Samiti. I was startled to realize that the Tenida stories I had read for their accounts of Kolkata spoke of a city that never was, and a way of life that existed only in the author's imagination. Perhaps they were created from the same desire that binds us to these stories today: to escape from reality into a life and language richly satisfying, through made up of the simplest ingredients.

As it stands, this translation represents only a small fraction of the Tenida stories, and an even smaller part of Narayan Gangopadhyay's oeuvre. I began by translating whatever I remembered having most enjoyed reading. Logical principles of selection tend to fail when faced with such a large set of stories, varying in plot but uniform in appeal to anyone who has ever sympathized with Pela's sickly spleen or wondered about the contents of the Great Gloomyswami's mysterious pot. For tales like these, the only reasonable—and satisfying—expedient is to translate them all. Tenida is a project to which I will always want to return.

Many people have helped to bring this book into being. My parents undertook the unenviable task of reading Tenida aloud to a refractory six or seven year-old me. My father even had a special voice for the Great Gloomyswami. Like all my other projects, this translation was begun, battled with and finished because of their support, and the encouragement of my brother Siddhartha. My sincerest thanks to Shri Nirendranath Chakraborty who, in addition to providing approximate dates for the early stories, recounted his memories of living close to the author's home on Potoldanga Street. Shri Arijit Ganguly not only gave me permission to translate his father's works but patiently answered my questions about them and their author, even going to the trouble of consulting family records. I owe him a special debt of gratitude.

Aparna Chaudhuri was born in Kolkata. She studied English literature at Jadavpur University and the University of Oxford, and is currently a graduate student at Harvard. Her translation of Rabindranath Tagore's Shey *was published as a* Penguin Modern Classic *in 2007. She enjoys reading, travel and music, and has been trained in classical dance and martial arts. She hopes to return to Kolkata after her studies are complete, and to pursue a career that combines teaching, research and translation.*

The Best of Tenida

CONTENTS

NAME: Narayan Gangopadhyay, born Taraknath Gangopadhyay
BORN: 8 February 1918 in Baliadingi, Dinajpur
FATHER: Pramathanath Gangopadhyay
MOTHER: Golapibala Devi
EDUCATION: He studied Bengali literature at Kolkata University, and came first in the MA examinations. He later earned a doctorate for his work on the short story.

LITERARY CAREER

Though Tenida is perhaps his best-loved creation, Narayan Gangopadhyay wrote many other kinds of fiction—short stories, novels and plays—as well as poetry and essays. He won fame with his first published novel, *Upanibesh* (The Colony). His works include the novels *Timir-tirtha* (Journey into Darkness), *Alo'r Sarani* (The Path of Light) and *Beetangsha* (The Snare). He also authored plays such as *Bhadatey Chai* (Lodgers Wanted) and *Agantuk* (The Stranger) and several collections of short stories.

GROWING UP

Most of the Tenida stories are set in Kolkata. But the author grew up far away from the city, in the village of Baliadingi in north Bengal. In *Amar Katha* (My Story), a short autobiography, he lovingly describes his birthplace:

> I was really very young then. My home was in a very beautiful part of Dinajpur district. The blue waters of the Atrayi River went rippling past our house, bearing their freight of huge trading ships and *shimul* flowers like

little red lamps. Two *krishnachura* trees stood on either side of our front door—when they bloomed, it seemed as if someone had spread a red and yellow carpet below. A little further away, rows of *bakul* trees filled the air with their fragrance.

My days passed in the shade of that bakul grove. At night, I lay watching the will-o'-the-wisp flicker far away, on the marshy shores of the lotus pond. Grandmother used to say the light came from headless spectres, each with a glowing cyclops' eye on its chest, its arms outstretched to trap prey. Shuddering at that distant light and listening to Grandmother's fairytales, I would fall asleep without knowing it.

Young Narayan's literary interests were fostered by his father, a police officer by profession, and a passionate lover of books. He subscribed to many papers and journals, including a host of children's magazines—*Khokakhuku, Sandesh* (the magazine founded by Upendrakishore Ray and edited for several years by his son Sukumar), *Mouchak* and *Shishu-shathi*. An eager and precocious reader, Narayan soon turned from *Khokakhuku* to his father's literary papers, devouring Saratchandra Chattopadhyay's novel *Srikanto,* first serialized in the magazine *Bharatbarsha.*

Narayan Gangopadhyay began writing for children when he was just a child. His first reader was his friend Sudhin, and here is the story of how Sudhin helped Narayan to become a writer.

By then I had read quite a few of the adventure stories in the *Ananda-lahari* series. The idea of a crime novel set fire to my imagination. In my one-person literary world, I produced an illustrated paper. If I remember correctly, its name was *Chitra-Bichitra*. It comprised eight quarter-sheets of foolscap paper. I alone was editor, artist, author, publisher and reader. There were three poems, an editorial and an exciting tale of mystery and adventure, with three grisly murders in its very first instalment. This was my first long story or novel.

There in our house in Dinajpur, where thick-leaved mango trees cast their shade and the fragrance of sweet-lime blossoms floated in through the windows, where thirty-six kinds of pickle stood drying in tall glass jars in the courtyard and Budhni, our Santhal maid, washed dishes by the well, huge silver earrings in her ears and a cross expression on her face, where a ear-splitting din from Dada's room told us that he was practising music—there, in that very ordinary Bengali household, I sat perched atop a rugged mountain of packing boxes and lost myself in filling up two and a half pages of foolscap paper with guns, bombs, secret chambers and savage murders. Can you imagine it? But I went on writing. Who could stop me?

Then, one day, I was caught. The late Rabindranarayan Ghosh, erstwhile principal of Ripon College, had only one son, Sudhin Ghosh, nicknamed Santu. He was my best friend. One day he came over to invite me to a game of marbles. 'Come on,' he said.

I said, 'No, I'm writing a story.'

'A story!' Sudhin was dumbfounded. For a while, he just couldn't believe it. 'Let me see it,' he said at last.

I read out one instalment of my novel from *Chitra-Bichitra*. What a sudden change came over him! I realized his eyes were sparkling with excitement. He had completely forgotten about the marbles. 'What happened next?' he asked eagerly.

I answered with the dignity of an editor, 'You'll know in the next instalment.'

'How much is a monthly subscription to your paper?' asked Sudhin.

'You'll find all the rules written out in it,' I said. 'Advertisements are two annas a page, one anna for half a page. A yearly subscription will cost you four paise, postal charges included.'

Sudhin immediately put his hand in his pocket. Bringing out the half-anna he had saved to buy fried gram, he announced, 'I'll subscribe.'

I don't remember how long I went on producing that paper. Nor can I recall if my adventure story was ever finished. But Sudhin went away one day, to live in Kolkata with his father and be educated there. That was probably the end of both paper and story.

I never saw him again, only read of the death of 'sportsman Sudhin' in the papers much later. But I haven't forgotten my first reader yet, and never will. Over the course of my life, I've made many friends. Perhaps some of them have even enjoyed reading my work. But the blind admiration of my childhood friend is something I'll never find again.

Friendship is the essence of the Tenida tales. However much Tenida bullies Pela, Habul and Kyabla, the four boys from Potoldanga are almost always to be found together. They go to school, pass (and fail) exams, chat over snacks, sitting on the Chatterjees' front step and go on holidays in a group.

As the eldest of the four and the leader of the gang, Tenida is respectfully called 'dada' (shortened to 'da', meaning 'elder brother' in Bengali) by the others. Bengali fiction has other famous 'dada'-figures as well:

GHANADA: Ghanashyam Das, Ghanada to the other inhabitants of his boarding house (*mess-bari*) at 72 Banamali Naskar Lane, was created by Premendra Mitra in 1945. A practised teller of tall tales, Ghanada always appears ensconced in his armchair at the mess-bari, filching cigarettes from his audience. But his stories take him all around the world, from the Japanese island of Sakhalin where he battles a man-slaying mosquito, to the red soil of Mars on an intergalactic adventure. Like Tenida, Ghanada is fond of his food. He polishes off rich mutton curry, chutney, curd and sweets at a single meal, while his friends bribe him to join their meetings with *beguni, hinger kochuri* and prawn cutlets.

FELUDA: Satyajit Ray's famous detective first appeared in the short story 'Feluda'r Goendagiri', published in *Sandesh* in 1965. Though his real name is Pradosh Chandra Mitter, he is Feluda to his young cousin and constant companion, Topshe. Lalmohan Ganguly, who writes sensational stories under the pen name of Jatayu, frequently joins the cousins on their adventures. Modelled on iconic detectives of English fiction, such as Sherlock Holmes and Hercule Poirot, Feluda relies chiefly on brainwork to solve his cases. But he is also an expert in martial arts, and in the use of his .32 Colt revolver. He also enjoys the good life—books, travel, adda, Charminar cigarettes and of course, tasty snacks.

TENIDA'S KOLKATA

Tenida and his friends live in the Kolkata of the 1940s. Potoldanga, their neighbourhood, is right in the heart of the city, close to College Street. Though not really brought into focus, the atmosphere of the city, the architecture of its buildings and the life on its streets form an important dimension of the stories. The four usually gather on the Chatterjees' *rowak* (a raised platform running along a house-front, still to be seen in many old north Kolkata buildings). From their place on the rowak, neither in the house nor on the street, Tenida and his cohort sample the sights, sounds and, most importantly, the tastes of the city, buying alu kabli, chops, savouries and jhalmuri from nearby vendors. At the same time, they remain within a local and domestic frame. Family members (such as Tenida's formidable Borda) and family occasions (like Kyabla's uncle's visit at the beginning of *Charmurti*) are frequently mentioned. Potoldanga itself appears to be the major unit of community life—the four constantly stress their loyalty to their neighbourhood and are members of the Potoldanga Thunder Club.

Do you belong to a local club? Have you ever performed a play in your neighbourhood, like Tenida and his friends in 'Sage Dadhichi, Lord Viswakarma and Lots of Little Bugs'?

TENIDA AND HIS TIMES
National and regional spirit also runs high. The early stories were written just around the time India gained independence. We are told that Tenida frequently beats up 'Tommies' (British soldiers) on the Maidan—an amusing detail, but suggestive of turbulent

times. The stories also give us a sense of the changing political geography of Bengal, divided at this time into West Bengal and East Pakistan (now Bangladesh). Tenida's loyalties seem to lie with West Bengal. At the same time, Habul Sen, who comes from Dhaka and speaks in the East Bengal dialect, is his close friend. The Tenida stories never allow references to political turmoil to spoil their fun. Rather, friendship is shown to erase differences.

Food, talk and Tenida

Tenida may have the biggest appetite, but all four friends are passionate about food. No meeting is complete without a snack, often consumed by Tenida alone. This preoccupation with food of all kinds, from delicacies like prawn cutlets to the weak catfish curry that sustains Pela in his bouts of malaria, gives the stories their quintessentially Bengali flavour. Bengalis are famously fond of eating, a tradition that popular literature makes much of. Think of Sukumar Ray's evergreen collection of poems entitled *Khai-Khai* (Let's Eat).

Adda, the Bengali word for a chat, is another key ingredient in the flavour of the stories. The Tenida tales conjure up a world of leisure, where the four boys can sit endlessly on the Chatterjees' rowak, exchanging stories, planning holidays, rehearsing plays and eating a bewildering variety of snacks. Studies and examinations fade into the background. We just know that Tenida has failed every exam possible!

Are 'adda' and good food important parts of your life? How much can you relate to the laid-back, easy-going lives of Tenida, Pela, Habul and Kyabla? Is it possible to have friends as close as they are to each other, even without as much time to spend together?

GLOSSARY

akanda: a wild shrub with clusters of white or pale lavender flowers

amra: a fruit with a leathery skin and tart pulp

Aniket: one of the names of Lord Shiva. Literally meaning 'homeless', it is generally construed as 'omnipresent', or 'one who resides in the entire world'.

alu kabli: a spicy snack made chiefly of potatoes, a very popular street food in Kolkata

basak (leaves): the leaves of the shrub *Adhatoda vasica,* famous for their medicinal properties, especially in curing bronchial disorders

beedi: an Indian cigarette made of tobacco wrapped in a leaf

besan: gram flour, often made into a paste with water and used as a coating for fried foods

Bhanumati: a medieval queen reputed to have been a very powerful magician

chamchikey: a species of small bat

chanachur/dalmoot: a popular Bengali snack, a spicy mixture of fried lentils, nuts, and sometimes curry leaves.

Dadhichi: an ancient and much-revered Hindu sage. Legend says he sacrificed his life so that the gods could make weapons from his bones to destroy the demon Vritra.

dak bungalow: Dating from colonial times, dak bungalows were rest houses built along the main district roads and postal routes, primarily for the use of government officials but available to other travellers for a fee.

Durbasa: an ancient Hindu sage, feared for his bad temper. Some classical sources say that he was born from Shiva's wrath, hence his irascibility.

gandal (leaves): the leaves of a plant otherwise known as Gandhabhadali, used for curing stomach disorders

ghagra: a traditional embroidered skirt mostly worn by the women of North and West India

Ghanada: a fictional character created by the Bengali writer Premendra Mitra

ghentu: a wild shrub with some medicinal properties

ghugni: another snack popular in Bengal, made of dried yellow peas cooked in a spicy gravy, often topped with fresh chopped onions, chillies and coriander leaves

golguppa: also known as *phuchka* in Bengal. A very popular street food, it consists of a crisp round shell made of flour or semolina, filled with a spicy mixture of potatoes, chillies and tamarind-flavoured water.

Hari bol: an exclamation meaning literally 'Take the name of the Lord!' Hari is one of the names of the Hindu god Vishnu.

Ilbal: Hindu mythology tells of two demon brothers, Vatapi and Ilbal. Vatapi, who had the power to assume any form he desired, would kill people by assuming the shape of a goat, being eaten by them, and then tearing his way out of their stomachs when Ilbal called his name. The sage Agastya finally destroyed Vatapi by digesting him before Ilbal could summon him back to life.

Indra: the supreme deity, and ruler of heaven in Hindu mythology

jadyapaha: a Sanskrit word rarely used in Bengali, meaning 'remover of inert ignorance'

jhalmuri: a popular roadside snack made of puffed rice (muri) mixed with spices, nuts, chopped onions and chillies

kabuliwallah: an itinerant trader, from the north-west of the subcontinent if not actually from Kabul (Afghanistan)

Kailash: Though there is a real Mount Kailas in Tibet, the reference here is to the mythical mountain on which Lord Shiva is believed to reside, with his consort Parvati.

kalmi: a trailing vine that grows at the edges of ponds and streams. It is edible, and known as 'water spinach' in English.

Kathamala: a collection of fables compiled in the late nineteenth century by the famous social reformer, Ishwar Chandra Vidyasagar

khichdi: a dish made by boiling rice and lentils together

khokababu/khoka: an affectionate Bengali term used for a small boy. Because of his nasal intonation, Seth Dhunduram pronounces *khoka* as *khonka*.

khoya: a sweet condiment added to tobacco

kirtan: a kind of devotional song

Kishkinda: the kingdom of the monkeys in the Ramayana

kul: a berry-like seasonal fruit, from which sweet and sour pickles are made

ledikenis: deep-fried balls of cottage cheese soaked in syrup, a popular Kolkata sweet

motichur: a variety of laddu

Mainak: a mythical mountain

Mohonbagan: a famous Kolkata football club

Mughlai paratha: a rich flatbread stuffed with eggs and sometimes meat, a popular street food in Kolkata

nagrai: traditional Indian shoes with upturned toes

palash: a tree bearing a vibrant red flowers, often called 'flame-of-the-forest'

polta (leaves): the edible leaves of the *potol* or pointed gourd plant, used in some traditional Bengali dishes

potol: a vegetable very common in Bengal. Known as *parwal* in North India, it has no real English name, though it is sometimes called 'pointed gourd'.

rajbhog: a sweet made of balls of cottage cheese soaked in sugar syrup; a more decadent version of the rasagolla

rudraksha: The dried berries of this tree are used to make rosary-like chains prized by devout Hindus.

Shantanu: The reference is probably to the mythical sage Shantanu, whose wife Amogha gave birth to the Brahmaputra River. The Mahabharata, however, mentions another Shantanu— the king of Hastinapur and husband of the beautiful Satyavati.

shaora: a kind of tree very common in Bengal. It features frequently in ghost stories as the preferred abode of certain kinds of spirits.

sheekh/shammi kabab: varieties of kabab. Sheekh kababs are roasted on skewers, while shammi kababs are rounder, and made of a mixture of meat and ground chickpeas.

shukto: a slightly bitter vegetable curry, usually eaten at the beginning of a traditional Bengali meal

Trishanku: an ancient prince whose story is told in the Ramayana. He wished to ascend to heaven in his mortal body, but was forced to remain suspended between heaven and earth.

Vaishnav: a devotee of Lord Vishnu. The Vaishnavs are a major Hindu sect.

Vatapi: a mythical demon. See 'Ilbal'.

Viswakarma: a Hindu god, believed to be the divine engineer of the universe and the patron deity of all craftsmen

Read More in Puffin Classics

The Rhythm of Riddles:
Three Byomkesh Bakshi Mysteries

Saradindu Bandyopadhyay

Translated from the Bengali by Arunava Sinha
Introduction by Dibakar Banerjee

Classic whodunnits for crime fiction addicts

Saradindu Bandyopadhyay's immortal detective Byomkesh Bakshi has enjoyed immense popularity for several decades. From being a household name in the Calcutta of 1930s, when he was first created to a popular face on TV in the 1990s, Byomkesh along with his friend-cum-foil Ajit are perhaps the best loved of India's literary detectives. This collection brings together three of his classic whodunnits.

From a murder in a boarding house with too many suspects, to a mystery with a supernatural twist, and then busting a black marketeering ring in rural Bengal, the stories in this volume take the super sleuth to different locales on his quest for truth, and bring out his ingenuity and astuteness.

Translated into English for the first time by award-winning translator Arunava Sinha, the breathless pace and thrilling plots of these action-packed adventures will win Byomkesh a new generation of admirers.